"Look," Rate said tiredly, "We're in the navy. Couldn't you just skim over the pep talk and tell us who you want to kill?"

"The Council of Nicaea."

Joe stared in disbelief. "All of them?" he finally managed.

"You don't have to kill anybody. We just want to disrupt the council and alter the outcome."

"Jesus!" Gorson erupted.

"You won't have any trouble with him," the Director said. "Dead several hundred years by the time you're headed for."

TO SAIL THE CENTURY SEA

G.C. EDMONDSON

SF
ace books
A Division of Charter Communications Inc.
A GROSSET & DUNLAP COMPANY
51 Madison Avenue
New York, New York 10010

TO SAIL THE CENTURY SEA

An ACE Book

First Ace printing: July 1981
Published Simultaneously in Canada

2 4 6 8 0 9 7 5 3 1
Manufactured in the United States of America

Chapter 1

In the years since it had happened Rate had managed, if not to forget, at least not to think constantly of how large a part he had played in destroying the world he had known and hoped for. He knew now that he should have kept his mouth shut and never tried to convince anyone—especially anyone in the navy—that a United States Ship had . . .

Once a ship had turned out for Saturday inspection with tattered sails, scruffy and unpainted, lacking every important item of equipment. Surely if he and the men had worked at it they could have come up with some more believable excuse than a time warp. Lately Rate found it increasingly difficult to believe that himself.

But that many years ago nobody would have predicted any of the improbable events about to happen: imperial presidencies, unwinnable wars, criminal and insane politicians arrogating the purple to the oval office . . . . It was a lousy world. Knowing he had done his share to make it that way did not render Rate's days more endurable or his nights less insomniac.

The phone buzzed.

Rate passed a distracted hand through thinning hair and continued staring out the third floor window. Here inside his office he was spared having to look at the hideous concrete pile that was HQ NAVPAC. He gazed unseeing at catamarans and day sailers, the occasional power boat that gadded merrily up and down the bay, threading between fuel-restricted ranks of motionless destroyers at mooring buoys. Aboard the destroyers bored sailors trained every available lens on the glistening suntans of each yacht's female complement.

It had been years since Joe Rate had gone sailing. Each time he almost got up enough gumption to try it his midsection would remind him that he was over 30 now, and that some things can not be expected to work a second time. "Nevermore," he said to the mirror tinted window.

The door opened. It was his yeoman. His yeo*person*. Damned recruiters enlisted them with heady, used-car-salesman promises and then couldn't even come up with something comfortable to call the poor girls.

"Joe?"

He turned.

Yeoperson 1st Class Margaret White ran the office and did most of Joe's work. She was slim and competent. She was blonde. She was attractive. She was twenty-five. "I think you'd better be in," she warned.

He picked up the phone. "Rate here."

"Lieutenant Commander Joseph Rate?"

Joe had been in the navy long enough to sense rank without having to see the gold braid on an admiral's sleeves. "Yes, sir."

"Captain of the yawl *Alice*?"

"Not for a long time." Joe said. "But yes, sir, I did command her."

"An unusual voyage, as I recall."

Joe began to suspect when last he had heard this voice. "Commander Cutlott?"

"You got the name right but it's admiral now."

Mute moldering Mahan, Joe thought. *They're going to rake it all up again!*

"Busy?"

"Well sir." Joe lied, "It always gets hairy when it's time to write fitness reports."

"Let your yeoman do that," the admiral said. "We need you this evening in Washington."

"This evening?" Across the office Yeoperson White saw the agony in Joe's face. Wordlessly, she brought him a bottle of Maalox. Joe thanked her with his eyes and gulped to calm the churning in his stomach.

"You won't have to take a commercial flight." Admiral Cutlott was saying. "Just get over to the island before 1400 and there'll be a MATS plane waiting."

It was the middle of July, when Washington is slightly less habitable than Joe's memories of monsoon on the Mekong. "We're shorthanded and really buried here." He gave it the old college try.

"Who isn't?" Admiral Cutlott observed. "See you this evening about—2300 local time."

"Yes, sir. Be nice to see you again," Joe lied.

"What is it?" Yeoperson White asked when he had hung up.

Joe didn't know. More accurately, he hoped he didn't know.

"Joe, is there anything I can do to help?"

"Don't get in the habit of calling me Joe," he said. "It should only slip out once in a while when you're not thinking and then you should be embarrassed."

Yeoperson White gave him an odd look. "You're right," she said. "Understatement is the secret of all good acting."

"Take care of the place."

"But when will you be back?"

Joe shrugged.

She offered the Maalox again. Joe hesitated for an instant, then put the bottle in his pocket.

Riding the water taxi across the bay, he surveyed acres of

, undraped skin—some still taut and attention-getting. Which made him realize abruptly that he had never seen his yeoperson in less than uniform-of-the-day. She had long legs and a slim, well engineered body. Too bad. It was totally unjust. But at least it wasn't costing him anything. Probably doing him some good in these paranoid times.

The navy had always had a problem. Before coed days the problem had at times been uglier. But did the evil old men who made the rules have not even a vestigial memory of what it was like to be young?

Joe had come to his office one morning to find Yeoperson White already there, hunched in a corner and in tears. She was twenty-five, a serious young woman interested in her career. On the strength of an anonymous accusation from some seventeen-year-old enraged because she was not turned on by pimples, Yeoperson White was being investigated for lesbianism.

For Joe it had not been 100% altruism. Since his life and his career had gone so totally wrong years ago he had tried. Some girls had been charming. Some had been willing.

None had been Raquel.

Joe didn't want to know if Yeoperson White also struggled to forget someone. He didn't much care whether she fancied boys, girls, or St. Bernards, so long as she didn't fancy him.

They started leaving the office together, being seen together in those watering places where people go to be seen. It put an end to accusations and investigations and the poor girl was allowed to live in peace. It also scotched a few incipient suspicions about L.Cdr. Rate's lack of interest in the usual seafaring man's shoretime pleasures.

Joe and his yeoperson made wry jokes about 'living a lie' and evenings he walked her to the women's barracks on his way to BOQ, planting an occasional chaste kiss if an audience demanded it. And they managed to remain friends. He could trust her to keep papers from getting lost until he returned from whatever wild goose chase Commander—*Admiral*—Cutlott had dreamed up this time.

Joe wondered just what on earth could demand his undistinguished presence in Washington after all this time. As if he didn't know!

The MATS plane was a surprise. Instead of the usual lumbering C-47 he was herded aboard a widebodied jet so newly chartered that it still bore the smiling logo of a commercial airline. But the coffee and the gristly ham sandwiches were navy, as well as the harried girl who patrolled the aisle with plastic cups and a thermos-pitcher. Joe had released his seat back and was squirming as he searched for some hope of sleep. Twenty three hundred, for the love of Poseidon! Even if the time differential turned it into only eight pee emm for Joe's queasy stomach, what could possibly be this important?

Reviewing his blighted career Joe knew that only one thing he had ever done was that important. And then nobody had believed him. Why dig it all up now? If he could just get this blasted arm rest to fold up he could stretch out across two seats and . . . and somebody was coming to sit next to him.

The man who was stuffing a flight bag into the overhead rack wore the crow with special markings of the new super-chief rank that had not existed when Joe was an ensign. He was a thickset, muscular man with a shock of graying reddish hair. As Joe looked up the chief glanced down. They recognized each other at once. "Gorson." Joe said.

"Joe, my God it's been—" Then abruptly the chief was as glum as Joe. "I should have known," he said as he sat down. "Any more of us aboard?"

"I don't know how many are even alive."

"Me neither," the older man said. "Bastards really split us up. Where you been?"

"The 'Nam, the numb, you name it."

"I been in the Med with the 6th." Gorson's eyes narrowed. "Keep my seat." he said, and went to prowl the plane. Moments later he returned with a gaunt Tenneseean in tow. "Guess who's been planning menus in the Indian Ocean," the chief said.

"Hello, Cook," Joe greeted.

"Howdy, Mr. Rate. You s'pose they gonna give us all a medal?"

"You'd better put on a flack jacket before they pin it on," Rate said. Gorson and Cook glanced about nervously. The good old days when it was safe to gripe openly had passed. "Don't worry," Rate reassured them. "We're needed again."

"You really think so?"

Joe just looked at the chief petty officer.

Gorson sighed. "Two of us is possible. Three on the same plane is no damned coincidence."

"When'd you make superchief?" Rate asked.

This time it was the gaunt Tennesseean whose eyes narrowed. He studied the new crow sewed on an old, half wornout uniform, then glanced down at his own sleeve. "All them years," Cook mused, "and then all at once . . . Mr. Rate—?"

"About three weeks ago," Joe admitted. "Just short of getting passed over for the third time."

There was an embarrassed silence. Everybody knew what happened to an officer passed over three times for promotion. Gorson glanced over his shoulder and changed the subject.

Joe learned that both his second in command and his cook had raised their families and would soon be grandparents. "You married, Mr. Rate?" Cook asked.

Rate shook his head.

"She was quite a woman," Gorson began, then halted as abruptly as if someone had kicked him in the ankle.

"You going to accept?" Cook asked.

"Accept what?" Rate was tired and he knew the business at the other end was going to drag on most of the night. He wished he could sleep. The plane gave a premonitory bobble and he was relieved when the 'fasten seat belts' sign came on. "We'll have time to work it out when we get there," he said as Cook turned to find his seat. He corkscrewed himself around into some semblance of comfort and closed his eyes.

But he could not sleep.

They had not believed him then. In spite of total congruence among the crew's debriefings the navy had wavered between malingering and collective hallucination. For someone to rake it all up after all these years could only mean one thing.

Chapter 2

''The Russians are experimenting,'' Admiral Cutlott said.

It was an unusual session. The admiral and a suitable entourage of brass, flanked by three civilians, sat on one side of the conference table. On the other side, facing the admirals and civilians, were those members of Joe's original crew aboard the *Alice* who could still be scraped up by navy computers. All three of them.

Back when Ensign Rate had done the donkey work for civilian scientists, furnishing a woodenhulled and non-magnetic platform propelled by sails instead of humping, thumping engines, it had been a typical day of lowering transducers and setting off TNT charges at various distances while doubledomes listened and devised ways to detect enemy submarines. No one had planned on something going wrong and sending the *Alice* and her people through Viking and Roman and prehistoric times. Officially, it had never happened.

Joe's people had survived the elements, natural disasters,

and the hazards of battle. They had brought their ship and their flag home. Instead of a hero's welcome they had achieved loss of pay, restrictions of liberty, and an enduring cloud that had dampened many careers. Had it not been for some foolhardy heroisms in the 'Nam that had been caught on the six o'clock news Joe might still have been only an ensign.

"The Russians have been experimenting," R. Adm. Cutlott repeated.

Several replies occurred to Joe but he saw little point in opening old wounds.

"Experimenting with time travel invented by me and Cook and offered free to our own government years ago?" Chief Petty Officer Sig Gorson felt no compunction about rubbing their noses in it. From the stilted manner of Gorson's delivery Joe could guess how many sleepless, teethgritting nights the chief had spent waiting and preparing for this moment.

"I got my thirty in next month," Cook added. "Be danged if I can figure why nobody ever thunk up a re-up bonus for a good cook."

The collective displeasure of a rear admiral, four captains, and a commander was vitiated by a yeoman who grinned behind a hastily raised steno pad.

"If this session goes much past my bedtime I too may opt for an early retirement," Joe said.

"But we need you!" the commander blurted. He was about to say more when he noted the hard and cold looks of those on his side of the table.

"What we need," one of the captains explained, "Is a man with some knowledge of languages and history."

And time travel. "I haven't resigned my commission yet," Rate said tiredly. "Whose grandfather is to be the first victim of retroactive Russian assassination?"

Suddenly everyone on the other side of the table was talking. "Now maybe you'll believe The Man when he says we need plumbers!" Admiral Cutlott's shrill voice overrode the rest.

"Where did you hear that?" the senior captain demanded.

Joe stared, wondering if this could be for real. *"Hear it?"* he asked. "Has the Imperial Palace lost all faith in American ingenuity?"

"You just thought that up on the spur of the moment?"

"It has been a very long moment. And it also struck me as the first thing that would come to mind if—" Joe abruptly edited himself. "—if certain people were to acquire a working time machine."

"Did you ever—?"

"I did not." Joe said firmly. "Quite apart from the dangers inherent in any paradox, there is a natural prohibition to that particular use of time machines."

"You talk like there was some kind of crime involved."

"The precise term," Joe said, "is *premeditated murder.*"

"My God!" somebody muttered, "A moralist!"

"Ain't havin' nothin' to do with it!" Cook said.

The door opened and a nervous marine ported his automatic weapon, then spun it to a "present arms" as he recognized the dark mustached, dark haired man who strode to the table. Joe Rate had never seen the Director before but recognized him instantly from countless TV shots. He felt a faint intermingling of triumph and awe as he got his first real look at the odd planes and angles of that longheaded, narrowjawed almost-handsome face. It was the face of a victorian explorer—the ascetic fanaticism that would go to the ends of the earth if that was what it took to get away from a devoted wife. It was the face of moral majority—of a True Believer.

The Director came straight to Joe Rate, smiling and extending a hand as he approached. "So you're the one who did it. I've wanted to meet you for years." As he continued talking Joe wondered how he had ever managed to dislike and mistrust this man. Finally the Director was sitting with the rest of the brass across the table. "The President takes a strong personal interest in the success of this project," he said. Gorson and Cook exchanged a look. Neither spoke.

"Since the President wishes success," Joe said, "I suppose the project will be pushed to a successful conclusion. But so far nobody's said exactly what we're going to do.''

One of the lesser captains picked up his cue to go into some involved randygazoo about the secrets act. Joe felt like reminding all hands that he too was a citizen of this same country, had been an officer in the same navy for several years. But if the navy had taught Rate nothing else, it had taught him to wait.

Gorson, whose retirement and pension were comfortably bombproof, had less patience. "We all know the Russians ain't nice," he said. "We all know there ain't a single friendly face around an oil well. What I don't know is why I'm being sworn to secrecy about what's on the six o'clock news."

Admiral Cutlott glared but did not reply. Joe recalled a time when nothing would have delighted Cutlott more than to keelhaul Gorson and Cook and probably Joe Rate too. "Look," he said tiredly, "We're in the navy. Couldn't you just skim over the pep talk and tell us who you want to kill?"

"The Council of Nicaea." It was the first time any of the civilians had spoken.

Joe stared in disbelief. "All of them?" he finally managed.

"You don't have to kill anybody. We just want to disrupt the council and alter the outcome."

"Jesus!" Gorson erupted.

"You won't have any trouble with him," the Director said. "Dead several hundred years before the time you're heading for."

"Two hundred ninety six by accepted chronology," Joe muttered.

"That can't be—" Abruptly the elderly graybearded civilian halted. He fiddled with a calculator, adding 4 to 325, subtracted 33, and gave Joe an awed look.

Joe was equally puzzled. An admiral, four captains, a commander, and three civilians whose names he'd heard and promptly forgotten were sitting here listening to dangerous, possibly world-destroying nonsense and nobody was even

—while he was struggling to make some sense from this brush with unreality Gorson summed it up. "We came back and the navy turned loose a bunch of high voltage shrinks to convince me I was hallucinating. I got to hand it to you though. You finally convinced me."

"You're not hallucinating, Chief," one of the captains said.

"Of course not," Gorson snapped. "But if you think I'm going back to kill somebody who might turn out to be one of my own ancestors then you've sure as hell been smoking something funny. I thought senior officers didn't do that."

"We're not going to kill anybody," the civilian repeated. "Just change a few minds and influence the voting."

"What the hell," Joe said airily. "It won't hurt *us*. We'll be the only people on this whole planet that won't be affected. If you're game I am."

"It's all been worked out very carefully," Admiral Cutlott said.

Joe began to realize these madmen in responsible positions were dead serious. They were going to turn him loose to destroy the world. *Worked out very carefully*. He considered what he ought to do. To refuse the mission would accomplish nothing. They would just turn it over to somebody with fewer qualms—somebody who could really screw it up. "We'll go," Joe said. "We're navy and it's our duty." What he did not add was that as Joe Rate saw his duty, the thing to do was take whatever equipment they issued him, jump into the middle of last week, and take infinite pains to make sure they did absolutely nothing.

"I knew you'd do it," the admiral said. "And this time you'll be starting out with proper equipment and arms."

Gorson and Cook were studying Joe with a blend of curiosity and horror. Joe rubbed his nose with his forefinger, wondering if either of his old shipmates would understand this time-honored gesture. Then he realized the brass across the table might know it even better. They ought to. They were the real con men.

The meeting was breaking up now that they were sure of

their men. "—briefing," one of the captains was saying. "And you won't be totally on your own this time. Dr. Greybull will be going along for the ride."

Joe's heart sank. Should have known they would never trust him alone. Greybull was the one who had whipped out a calculator and discovered that Joe knew how to add. He was a lean, beaky man with gray hair, gray beard, and a superficial resemblance to old Cousteau. But not, Joe guessed, with the oceanographer's respect for the environment. There would be a name for this kind of wrecker. If the world lasted long enough to understand the damage such people could do Dr. Greybull might go down in history as the world's first tempolluter.

Chapter 3

"Nice touch," Gorson said with a hint of sarcasm.

"Danged if she don't look just like the old *Alice*," Cook added as he eased his seabag from his shoulder down onto the dock.

Rate did not trust himself to speak. The *Alice* had been 89 feet of yawl in the classic yachting style, crafted of nothing but the best woods. When a news baron's accountants explained that the tax laws he had promoted also applied to him he had been forced to retrench, making the best of it by taking countless pages of self-congratulatory publicity on his superpatriotism, plus a tremendous tax shelter, when he gave the original *Alice* to the United States Navy. Stuck with a wooden ship in an era with no iron men, the navy had finally found use for the yawl as a vibration-free floating instrument platform.

The yacht before them looked very like the *Alice*, save that this was a ketch, with the mizzen stepped forward of the rudder post. It promised a balanced rig and easier sailing than had ever the *Alice* with that silly little jigger mast of her impractical yawl rig perched on the extremity of the fantail. There being a limited number of ways that space can be efficiently utilized belowdecks, Rate supposed the living quarters would be similar too.

That was what he dreaded. Joe had no more desire to see the old *Alice* again than does some legless, armless soldier yearn to revisit the scene of the crime. While Gorson and Cook hoisted seabags and trotted down the gangway, pausing and facing aft to salute the ensign, Joe lingered on the dock.

This hull had been fiberglassed, which made it stronger, and with fewer worries about dry rot or worms. On a little pulpit forward of the mainmast a small radar antenna poised ready to rotate. And foul the luff of an overlapping jib every time they came about.

The cabin top and deck were painted in some odd geometric pattern. Joe moved closer and saw the yacht was covered with solar cells. Something good had come from the petroleum shortage.

The old *Alice* had needed diesel fuel for the auxiliary engine, for making electricity, for the galley stove—for all the little amenities that had separated them from the timebound primitives with whom they had trafficked and fought and made love. Suddenly his stomach was twisting again.

It was hopeless. The world might be getting smaller every day but it was still too large ever to find one girl when the search was not just over a planet, but over a millenium as well. Besides, if that Dr. Greybull, who had been mindblown at the discovery that a lieutenant commander knew how to add . . . Joe struggled to look on the bright side of it. Maybe he could deep-six the scientist and blame it on . . . the Byzantines?

"Hey Joe, you comin' aboard?"

A pimply seaman with progressive ideas considered the spectacle of a whitehat cook calling a lieutenant commander "Joe" and wondered if he'd been transported to heaven.

"In a minute." Rate ignored the goggling seaman. He

walked the length of the dock to study the ketch from bow on. In spite of fiberglassing and fresh paint and a new stripe of boot topping to conceal harbor scum the resemblance was . . . His mind was playing tricks on him.

"Stores all aboard," Cook said when finally Rate lowered himself down through the cabin slide. "Wish we'd had all this freezedried stuff back when we 'uz livin' on raw sheep and rye."

Gorson came aft from poking about in the chain locker. "Good shape," he said. "Look familiar?"

Joe admitted that it did.

"Take a look in your cabin."

The high narrow bunk with drawers underneath was as Joe remembered. The rest of the cabin was taken up with a chart table and a bolted-down chair. He flipped the switch and a battery-powered fluorescent came on. Beneath the chart table was a drawer with a sextant and a celestial navigation calculator, along with plastic-sealed packs of extra batteries. Some doubter had included a slide rule just in case. Joe sat in the bolted-down swivel chair and sighed. Gorson stuck his head in the door.

"They changed the engines," he said.

"Oh?" Joe supposed he had really known it the first time he set eyes on this refurbished, fiberglassed, rerigged-from-yawl-to-ketch hull. This was no replica. He was back aboard the original *Alice*.

"No more diesel," Gorson continued. "Damned thing looks electric. Maybe we're going to string a long cord."

Joe remembered all the solar cells on cabin top and deck. He hoped they would not have any prolonged winter or cloudy weather. He flipped on the weather frequency, catching the end of "—night and morning low clouds, burning off by midday."

He began rummaging in the log, trying to learn how many men it took to crew the *Alice* now that she had been modernized and automated. He was still looking when there was a confused racket of shouting topside. He emerged from his cabin and climbed back up through the slide into the cockpit.

The man who had tossed a seabag ahead of him down into the cockpit was stocky and swarthy and Joe would not have known him if it were not for the eternal cigar that he cupped in his hand long enough to salute the ensign, then reinserted into his broad mouth, puffed vainly for a moment, and finally spat overboard. "I remember when you smoked them a lot shorter than that," Rate said.

Engineman Abe Rose grinned. "Those were the days my friend. Abruptly he halted and stared. "Mr. Rate! Is it . . ?" He recognized Gorson and Cookie. "I wondered why I suddenly got a promotion and big re-up bonus just when I'd finally made up my mind to quit."

Another man, seabag on his shoulder, was coming down the dock. "Freedy," Cook muttered. "That makes five of us."

Joe had not thought that many of them would have lasted this long—not after all the things the country and the navy had been through. "Welcome aboard," he told the radioman.

Freedy squinted, accepted the proferred hand, and finally fished out his glasses. "Mr. Rate?" he asked when he had them balanced precariously over his prominent nose. "I thought they'd killed you just like the rest of us."

"River boat in the delta," Gorson murmured. "I heard about it." From the querulous, old man's voice it seemed that Freedy might have little to offer this expedition of temporal retreads.

By evening Joe decided there would be no more of the old gang. He had three new kids whose total years in service would not approximate his own—and Joe Rate was still the new boy among the *Alice's* old hands. He felt sorry for the kids. If he was unhappy with them, what must the poor children feel about being dumped among all these superannuated relics from black powder and stone axe days? He prowled the *Alice* and saw they would not be crowded this time, there were two bunks left over. Then he remembered Dr. Greybull.

"When do we sail?" Gorson asked. Cookie had dished up evening chow and the crew lounged about the *Alice's* solar-celled deck picking their teeth.

"Orders say 0800," Joe said.

"Foul tide," Gorson growled.

"I don't imagine the navy pays much attention to tides any more."

"We're the only sailing ship in the whole lashup. Too bad we can't . . ." Gorson left it dangling.

"Yeah." Joe went below, made sure his calculator-alarm clock was set, and turned in. When he awoke the *Alice* was under way. He could feel the beginning of a gentle ground swell.

"What in hell is going on?" he demanded as he burst into the cockpit.

Gorson grinned. The *Alice* crept along past the jetty, helped by a favoring tide. It took Joe an instant to realize that it was not the near-silent electric motors that had awakened him. He had been aroused by the sound of a couple of the new boys hoisting the mains'l with an electric winch.

"You didn't really want that civilian along, did you?" Gorson asked.

"Of course not!" Joe admitted. "But I don't want to spend the rest of my life in the Portsmouth brig either. Come about and get back to the dock. NOW!"

"Yes, sir," Gorson grumbled. "Just a trial run anyhow to see how she handles with this new rig."

Joe decided not to make an issue of it. But he would not go back to sleep until the *Alice* was once more moored at her pier just inside Ballast Point. Not twenty-four hours aboard and already the honeymoon was over. He should have remembered Gorson. He did now.

As the *Alice* pulled up to a dock drenched in the ghastly glare of sodium vapor lights two men with suitcases came hurrying down the pier. "Where were you?" Dr. Greybull demanded.

"Shakedown run," Joe said. "What's the problem?

You're not supposed to be here till tomorrow morning."

"We were just on our way to get a helicopter," the younger man said accusingly.

Joe studied him and decided this one had also been at the conference with Admiral Cutlott in Washington. The younger man bore an odd resemblance to The Director. "I hope you're the last," Joe said.

"Why?" the younger man bristled.

Joe's dislike was instinctive. "In the days of my innocence," he said, "I let civilians hog every bunk while my men slept embracing torpedos. Approaching combat invariably released bunk space for enlisted personnel. Therefore, unless you take his place, the next civilian sleeps on the cabin sole."

Dr. Lilly gave Joe an unfathomable look but did not reply.

"Now, about this mission," Dr. Greybull began.

"Anyone else popping around to make sure we don't sneak off?" Joe's anger was heightened by the knowledge that Gorson had planned exactly what the civilians suspected.

"Nobody that I can think of." The older civilian had a neat gray beard and abundant hair of the same color. He seemed puzzled.

Joe turned to Gorson. "Cast off." Turning back to the civilians he added, "I see neither of you are sailors."

They were not, but were duly flabbergasted to discover that Joe knew.

"There's never any wind after dark in this part of California," Joe explained, "and there isn't enough engine aboard this bucket to make a dent in a foul tide. Either we move out now or your 0800 departure will actually begin about noon—twelve hours from now."

While the civilians went below the *Alice* began backing away from the pier. Joe shook his head. No sailor would ever bring spacewasting suitcases aboard a yacht. If he really wanted to blow the archaeologists' minds maybe he could arrange for the civilians' luggage to be lost in some prechristian Byzantine crypt. Joe shuddered. Was it age or bitterness that gave him such ideas?

Time travel . . . once he would have exchanged his soul for a well equipped expedition to resolve some of his pet theories. But only governments had money nowadays. Financing meant control and he knew damned well what the government was planning. Why couldn't they at least let him go in forewarned? Did they think he would sell out to the Russians?

Probably. Nowadays everyone was for sale.

The *Alice* moved out into the channel and bounced for a minute in the wake of a wallowing, heavy-laden tuna clipper. The fishing boat had a foreign flag. There was the grind-whirr of an electric winch as the *Alice's* mains'l began rising ghostly in the light of a gibbous moon. There was no wind but sails would steady the *Alice* and reduce the nausea of her corkscrewing progress through a ground swell. Gorson was still at the wheel. Joe stood beside him and studied the binnacle. In the distance he saw the blinking of the last channel buoy light. "You know where I am," Joe said, and went below.

Still abmicturated for having to turn around and pick up the civilians, Gorson gave him a stiff nod.

I'm old, Joe thought as he undressed. He was thirty-eight. *I'm tired*. There was truth in this—if he equated exhaustion with boredom. *I'm bitter*.

And there he had it.

For years after she—after the first mission aboard the *Alice* Joe had bent every official ear trying to get funds to go look for—more research into time travel. He had reminded himself several times each day that time is a paradox, that time is meaningless, that years of delay meant nothing—that he could learn to fine-tune the machine and pick her up only seconds after she had disappeared, that Raquel would not have ended her brief life in some shark-infested sea.

But no paradox could reverse the changes in Joseph Rate. His hair was thinning; his stomach in constant rebellion. He was pudgy. Would Raquel even recognize the wreck of her gallant young captain? "Hell to grow old," he muttered as he folded his shoregoing uniform and stowed it in the bottom of a drawer. Once he had left a jacket on a hanger and a week later the constant motion of a small boat had left huge holes where it rubbed.

Sitting on his bunk clad only in skivvies, he finally realized what was different. The vinyl was not as frigid on his bare feet as linoleum had always been. Perhaps the world had improved in some small ways. He opened the drawer and removed the manila envelope that was felt-penned SEALED ORDERS *to be opened only when under way.*

Chapter 4

It was no worse than he had expected. Dr. Greybull was the scientific director and would issue all orders except those directly concerning navigation and the safety of the ship. Dr. Lilly was a security expert and would lend a hand with special weapons if needed. Joe was plowing through a second and more thorough reading of the sealed orders when someone knocked and before he could answer the door opened. It was the younger civilian.

"The plumber, I presume," Joe said.

The man with the thin, oddly angled face nodded. There seemed no smile in this man and scant potential for whimsy. He looked, Joe decided, like a younger brother of The Director. But Joe had not expected him to admit to his profession quite so readily. "Looking for anything special?" he asked.

Lilly's head swiveled constantly, looking into odd corners like the surveillance light in some maximum security stockade. He focussed briefly on Joe, then seemed to look through him. "We're going to spend a lot of time together," he said.

"You expect this mission to take a long time then?"

"Don't you?"

Joe shrugged. "If something *has* to be done, you do it and get out as quick and clean as possible."

"It has to be done."

"It's always a great comfort to be positive."

"Six months ago a defector told us the Russians were building reinforced plastic-steel-concrete vaults too large for Soviet Hero coffins and too small to live in. It was his opinion that they were too heavy for space and were designed more to resist pressure from outside than the other way around."

"I suppose the purpose of these containers is classified."

"Now that the Russians know we know there seems to be an acceleration."

"What is it we're supposed to know?" Joe asked.

"The containers are about the right size for a fusion bomb and a detonator that could be set off by a seismic wave of the proper frequency."

"Seismic . . ?" Abruptly Joe saw where it was all going. "They jump back into prehistory and plant these where capital cities and other key installations will someday be?"

"The psychological profile *said* there was nothing wrong with your intelligence—just that your motivation was a little out of alignment."

Joe wondered what the plumber's psychological profile would have to say. "Do you believe it?" he asked.

"I believe you're intelligent."

"If I were a Russian I'd spread every cock and bull story I could invent just so the enemy would squander research and capital in wild goose chases."

"They have a time machine."

"Did they invent it or steal it?"

"You gave it to them."

Joe studied Dr. Lilly for a silent moment. "In any age less barbarous, that remark would allow me choice of weapons. Even in this thickskinned era—" Joe pondered his chances of doing something lethal before this expert could.

Lilly gave him a wolfish grin and did not change position.

After a moment the plumber said, "No one is accusing you of treason. But you spent years buttonholing everybody for funds. Even if you couldn't get the right people to listen, there *were* people listening very carefully all the time."

"Then why wasn't the subject classified?"

Lilly grinned again. "If *our* administration had been in you'd have been closemouthed or had your mouth closed."

Joe had thought himself beyond all politics or passion and yet this grinning fascist elicited a sudden choler so violent that his vision shimmered and the tiny cabin spun. Joe drew a careful breath and held it while clenching his teeth. He was navy. He was apolitical. Why did he so instinctively despise this man? Was he seeing in Lilly some dark reflection that he was unwilling to see in himself?

The *Alice* rolled with unexpected violence. They were still in the approaches to San Diego Bay and the traffic was heavy. With Gorson at the wheel, with radar targets up and with a floodlight on the mains'l there should be no danger. But Joe was captain. He passed through the weapons expert's private space on his way to the deck.

Just as he was sticking his head up through the cabin slide something came rasping over the *Alice's* stern quarter, scraping off the rail as it went. There was a crunch-craaaaack as the mizzen mast splintered, then the *Alice* was flung off course. The devastation swept back, dragging odds and ends overboard, leaving them alone in the darkness. Gorson raised his head from the bottom of the foot-deep cockpit and studied the splintered binnacle column and steering wheel. He expressed himself at some length.

The wheel was gone, the rudder jammed. "Where are we? What happened?" Joe demanded.

Gorson sprang to the electric winch controls to trim sails and try to haul the *Alice* back on course by sheer brute force. Behind them, disappearing in the pre-dawn darkness, was a fuel barge and presumably a tug up ahead towing it. Both tug and tow carried proper lighting. "Just passing Ballast Point," Gorson said over his shoulder.

Joe felt his insides shrivel. He squinted into the total

darkness, struggling to see the breakwater aport and the shoal a hundred yards astarboard. He could see nothing. The binnacle was wrecked and there was neither light nor compass. He studied the sky and cursed himself for not having consulted the nautical almanac. He had no idea where Orion ought to be this month. "What happened?" he repeated. Surely Gorson knew better than to dispute right-of-way with an unmaneuverable tow. "Didn't you see it?"

"I did not!" Gorson snarled. "One minute the channel was clear and the next that tug was behind us and the barge was ahead and the tow line was coming up over the stern." He glared around at the devastation. "Take weeks to patch it up," he growled. "And that damned tug wasn't—" He broke off as the ketch began falling off. There was not enough wind for steerageway but stars were wheeling as some tidal eddy pushed them toward shoal water.

Abe Rose erupted through the cabin slide and began fiddling with motor controls. By careful timing of his forwards and reverses, he got the unsteerable *Alice* back on her heading and pointed roughly seaward. "Can't stay here," he growled around his eternal cigar.

Joe was in total agreement. They were in the narrowest part of a busy channel. To stay adrift here, even if they could manage to keep off the rocks, could only end in collision with something larger than the *Alice* and too large to stop before wreath-throwing ceremonies were ended.

"Little more," Gorson muttered. "Now cool it." The mizzen mast was broken but he was struggling in concert with the engineman to steer the ketch by balancing the delicate push of engine with the still more delicate deflection of foresails against the ghost of a breeze.

"Damned tug was lit," Gorson growled when he and Rose had finally clawed past the invisible point and imminent disaster. "But a second earlier that lashup just *wasn't there*." He glared at Joe, prepared for an argument.

"You're right," Joe said. "It wasn't." He dived down the cabin slide, wondering how he had managed not to trample Dr. Greybull on the way up. Then he remembered the grayhaired scientist had been unpacking. The old man was still fiddling with an open suitcase atop the galley table. "Just what the hell do you think you're doing?" Joe demanded.

The open suitcase looked like a satchel bomb. Inside were dials and switches and a single glass cylinder somewhat larger than an old fashioned radio tube. "No point in wasting time," Dr. Greybull said. "I tried a short jump just for calibration—not over a century or so."

"In the channel of a busy harbor?" Joe's voice had risen an octave. He stared at the scientist, suddenly remembering that brief flicker when he had been talking with Lilly. Though he had been mad enough to bite nails that flicker-shimmer had not been pure rage.

"What does harbor or anywhere have to do with it?" Greybull asked.

"Who knows?" Joe said. "But you just managed to wreck us. We always tried to be well offshore before we tried anything."

"Did something go wrong? I thought all that noise was normal."

"If you want to see real abnormality just try slipping the cost of repairs into my operations budget!" Joe hurried back on deck to see what new troubles Gorson might be having. "Can you clear the breakwater?" he asked.

"I don't think we're even in the harbor any more," Gorson growled. "Do you feel that ground swell?"

Now that the bos'n mentioned it Joe did feel the unmistakable movement of shallow water in an open sea.

"That doubledome try out his new machine?" Gorson had broken out a portable boat compass and studied it with a flashlight. "Stars don't look right," he added.

Dr. Greybull stared at the shambles in the reflected glow of Gorson's flash. "Did we hit something?" he asked. "I had no idea this would happen."

Joe gave up squinting into the darkness and turned to the radar. The pips of several small fishing boats showed ahead but nothing lay in their direct path. Behind loomed the familiar Gibraltar-like outline of Point Loma, so no matter where their jump had taken them in time, they were still in sight of home.

"Already tried the radio, sir," Freedy said. "There's a lot of static and a little Morse but I can't raise any FM or single sideband."

"No TV?"

Freedy shook his head and pushed his glasses back up his nose.

Joe sighed. It was, he supposed, par for the course. Not half started and already the *Alice* was a wreck. He went back on deck and told Gorson where he thought they were.

"Back to San Diego for repairs?" Gorson asked.

"Can you imagine the splash we'd make in a navy yard with our funny uniforms and no BuShips documentation?"

"Yeah, I guess you're right. What you want to do?"

"Can you keep her sailing southwest away from land? Maybe we can come in behind some island or some uninhabited bay in Baja long enough to refit. At least, keep offshore till daylight and we can see how bad off we are."

"Right." Gorson began trimming sails. The mizzen was no longer working but the roller reefing and electric winches on the mains'l groaned no louder than usual. From the ease with which the chief got her to hold a heading Joe supposed the rudder was jammed in a near-neutral position.

Joe went below. Dr. Greybull was staring at the suitcaseful of dials and switches. "I'm most sorry about all this inconvenience—" he began.

"Save it," Joe said. "And in the future, if we have any, please don't turn any knobs without calling battle stations first. People too far out on the bowsprit tend to get left out of the jump. They end up swimming."

"My God!" Greybull muttered. "Why was none of this in the reports?"

"It was. People just chose not to believe them. It happened to someone rather close to me."

"Oh . . ?" Abruptly Greybull's face changed "Oh!"

Joe escaped into his cabin before he could be drowned in

sympathy. Greybull was a wellmeaning bungler. The unnerving Dr. Lilly was not. The world needed people like Lilly. But that couldn't make Joe like him any better.

When the old Director died there had been a Night of the Long Knives. By dawn the old blackmailer's career had been so thoroughly ventilated that nobody noted how, in the process, only *some* of the files had been burned.

The new Director came from the White House. But not very far from it. The new Director was safe: without ambition—with total loyalty to The Man who had been reelected three times with such ease that finally the whole wasteful farce of TV-predicted elections was declared superfluous—at least for so long as the Great Man should live. Americans loved their Imperial President. They'd better!

Joe fell into restless sleep trying to recall the exact wording to which he had sworn. Something about supporting and defending the constitution against all enemies, foreign and domestic. It had been a long time and he couldn't remember.

Morning came and all hands surveyed the disaster. There were broken stanchions but the cable that served as rail was still intact. Abe Rose assured Joe that, given time and good weather he could reweld the stanchions.

The major damage was the broken mizzen mast and steering gear. During the night Gorson and Rose had unhooked the cables from the shattered wheel column. The ketch was being steered from a makeshift tiller atop the rudder post extension. Rose *thought* that, given time, he could restore the steering gear. "But you'll never get the roller reefing to work on that mizzen mast again," he said. "We'll have to cut a new mast somewhere and go back to hand tieing reefs."

Gorson got work parties going and discovered that one of the new boys actually knew how to sew in reef points. He put him to work on the sail. Joe thanked whatever gods that the solar cells and most of the electrical gear seemed undamaged.

All morning the *Alice* rolled in calm seas with a hint of ground swell and not enough breeze to fill slack sails. After racketing diesels the faint whir of electric motors was uncanny. Joe noted that they now turned appreciably slower. He would have to ask Abe Rose just how long those batteries were good for. Then abruptly the motors resumed speed. It took Joe an instant to realize that Cook had just turned the electric galley stove off.

In faded denims and deck shoes the gray bearded Dr. Greybull was not quite the lubber he had seemed last night. "Have you any idea when we are?" he asked.

"No," Joe said.

"Have you checked the weather yet?"

Joe had not. "Are we supposed to look for lightning?" he asked.

"Afraid so. We've developed some capacitor storage that may work for short jumps—fine tuning to the exact year or month. But the power requirements for anything over a century seem to lie right in that awkward range—not quite enough to use up a fusion bomb, but more than any power plant can develop in a single surge."

Abruptly Joe understood what the doctor was getting at. "If the machine can manage short jumps without lightning," he said, "Then we can jump home and get repairs."

"There isn't time."

"You can *make* time," Joe said tiredly.

"It sounds logical but logic seems to have little to do with time travel."

"Our experience was that it took a power source like lightning to move back in time but we could practically bounce home."

"I know," the scientist said, "This apparatus seems to work the other way around."

"Sounds like you've been working on this for quite a while."

"Didn't you know?" Dr. Greybull shook his head. "Oppenheimer got classified out of his own work too." He glanced quickly around to see who was listening.

"But why, after all these years, am I suddenly back into it?"

Dr. Greybull's mouth opened. Hastily, he closed it and looked around again. "I've no idea, " he confessed. "It never occurred to me."

They were silent, gazing at the horizon. "Would you like to see the apparatus?" Greybull finally asked. "We've streamlined it a little. Only takes a minute to set up now."

"Our new fathometer is transistorized," Joe said. "No more vacuum tubes. Does that make a difference?"

"You were right about some resonance between the fathometer and that distillation coil in a partial vacuum. But we've consolidated it all."

"I thought you had your clothes in that suitcase."

Dr. Greybull was amused.

Joe concentrated on the horizon. They could not be more than a hundred miles south of San Diego and it was July and yet he saw a mass of clouds building up ahead. Maybe the paranoids were right and the Russians were playing with the weather. Those tropical disturbances kept moving farther north every year. The more exact term for those tropical disturbances was hurricane. Then he remembered that it had been July *before* the jump.

"It looks," Dr. Greybull observed, "Like we're going to get some action."

"Where were we really going?" Joe asked.

"Nicaea, 325 A.D."

"No way!" Joe said firmly. "Not until we've cut a new mast and finished repairs. Why do you want to go? Are the Russians burying something there?"

Dr. Greybull's look suggested that Joe was one of the paranoids. "What are you talking about?"

"Just repeating your friend."

Greybull glanced hastily around. "Dr. Lilly is no friend of mine!" he snapped.

Joe sensed that it was going to turn into a real fun trip. "Are you an historian?" he asked.

"Physicist." As Greybull saw Joe's disappointment he added, "But I confess to an incurable addiction to reading."

"What do you expect to do at the Council of Nicaea?"

"Does the Arian Heresy mean anything to you?"

"I've never taken a strong position about the number of angels can dance on the head of a pin, nor about *homoousios*," Joe said. "Seems to me the Church didn't think it out too well either until they were committed. Then they spent the next century manufacturing doctrine to fit that damned iota."

Greybull laughed. "Arius couldn't swallow that $3=1$ bit about the trinity. I wonder if he realized that his heresy turned Jesus into just another lower-case *deus* like any old pagan god."

"Apart from a few oddballs and freaks, who cares?" Joe demanded.

"The civilized eastern people have always been monotheists," Greybull said. "When the western barbarians started turning all their local spooks and fertility goddesses into saints, putting gods in every rock, the sophisticated easterners were outraged. They stayed estranged until a leader of their own came along to reaffirm monotheism."

"There is one god, whose name is God, and Muhammad is his messenger," Joe quoted. "They backed off from Christian spook raising and went right back to Jewish fundamentals. *Sh'ma Yisroel*–means the same thing."

"Except for the messenger," Greybull agreed. "But what might have happened if Arius had won and sent Athanasius back to Alexandria with his tail between his legs."

"A common east-west culture?" Joe guessed.

"With the Russians off in their neutral corner still crossing themselves with their own fourfingered heresy."

Joe gave a cracked laugh. "You really think that would work?"

"It has been worked out very carefully."

"I'll give you a hundred things could go wrong."

"That, I suppose, is why you're here."

"Devil's advocate? There are other and better historians. And speaking of devils, wouldn't you prefer the devil you know to the one you don't?"

"Speaking of devils," Greybull echoed.

The odd planes and angles of Dr. Lilly's head were emerging from the cabin slide. He was carrying a gun.

Chapter 5

Joe had seen too many people like Dr. Lilly. But despite years in the armed forces he had never seen a gun quite like the one the plumber bore. At first glance it was some kind of submachine gun. At least it bore a long, scimitar-curved magazine extending from its bottom. But the meter-long barrel had an offset sight so it could be aimed while the rearmost third of the barrel extended over a shoulder.

Lilly tossed a Wild Turkey bottle over the port rail and swung outboard of the shroud, hanging by one hand while he aimed the weapon with the other. When the bottle had been reduced to an occasional glint a hundred fifty meters astern he fired.

Smoke and brief puffs of orange flame spurted from the rear of the launcher as three projectiles exited the muzzle with machine gun rapidity. Joe had seen rocket pistols in the 'Nam, usually in the hands of some Ivy League type who did not trust his privileged existence to standard issue hardware. The pistols were elegant, longranged, with an extremely flat trajectory. Only when Ivy Leaguers began dying out of proportion to their limited numbers had it been discovered that, for jungle warfare, a wise man selects a weapon that does not leave a trail of fire and smoke pointing back to whence it was fired.

The Wild Turkey bottle disappeared along with a cubic meter of the Pacific, leaving Dr. Lilly with a tight satisfied smile as he swung back inboard.

"Have you any other weapons?" Joe asked.

"Several."

"I must respectfully request that you not fire that one aboard my ship again."

"Why?" The plumber was too startled for anger.

"You were careful this time but in real life situations people forget. The back blast from your repeater-bazooka can melt holes in dacron, or soften the ropes that keep those sails in place."

Dr. Lilly considered this for a moment, then nodded and went below. The next time he appeared on deck no weapons were visible. Joe considered suggesting that the plumber comply with navy regulations and jettison any more supplies of Wild Turkey, but there was little point. He was going to have trouble enough.

"Another hour."

"What?" Joe turned to Dr. Greybull.

"That disturbance is moving up fast." As the doctor spoke the *Alice's* canvas suddenly filled. She lay over on her lines and began sailing. The faint hum of electric motors rose half a note, then halted as Abe Rose turned off the power. One of the new boys was at the tiller. He looked questioningly at Joe.

"Point high," Joe said.

"Into that squall?" The boy's voice rose into unbelief.

"Get upwind of it or we'll spend the rest of our lives trying to outrun it." Joe studied the closehauled jenny that overlapped the luff of the mains'l. When the wind settled down they were going to be overcanvassed. The boy on the makeshift tiller was already struggling to compensate for the lack of a mizzen. Joe ordered the huge jenny taken in and replaced with a smaller jib.

Once the storm jib was set, he ordered the huge main replaced with a storm tris'l. The *Alice* now had roller reefing and electric winches, all controlled from the cockpit. Sails that had formerly flapped and torn fingernails and flung men overboard now rolled up as docile as window blinds—except that they now had a broken mizzen mast.

Joe went below to make sure everything in his cabin was tied down and/or stowed. Dr. Greybull had raised the fiddles on the galley table and was opening a suitcase.

Gorson and Cookie were studying the suitcase with a professional interest. Freedy seemed less old and frail today. The radioman sat wedged in a corner of the galley settee and squinted through thick spectacles. From the fo'csl a pair of the new boys peered with unreadable expressions.

"Stow it!" Joe said. "No playing with that machine until we're operational again." The new boys still stared. Abruptly Joe realized what was wrong. "Did anybody ever tell you—" He caught himself in time and did not call them "boys". "You new men what we're up to?"

Nobody had.

Jim Syverson was redhaired, freckled, and eighteen. Intelligence flickered across his open farmboy face. Howard Hennis was black, which would help Joe keep him straight from another Howard who had once sailed aboard the *Alice*. This Howard was tall enough for basketball. Gray-green eyes were not incongruous in his handsome, light brown face. He listened intently to Joe's briefing.

Gorson grinned. "Wonder what kind of broads we'll find this run."

Joe tried to ignore the sudden stab in his midsection. "Send the other boy down," he said. "They've a right to know what they're getting into."

"—you ain' chittin' us—sir?" the boy who had been steering asked. In spite of his surname, Kraus was swarthy and had the Spanish speaker's usual difficulty with any *sh* sound. "You really go back in *time*?"

"We did before," Joe said. "Unless somebody's screwed

up we will again the first time lightning strikes that thing Dr.
Greybull's putting away.''

"You gonna blow us up!'' Hennis said. "That man got
rockets aboard.''

Now why, Joe wondered, hadn't he thought of that? It was
his job. "Dr. Lilly!'' he bawled, "On the double!''

The security expert appeared with an abruptness that was
startling. More startling was that he stood at attention.

"What do you have in the way of electrically detonated
explosives?''

"Classified information, sir.''

"Okay by me if you want to play it that way,'' Joe said.
"But without a mizzen we're not pointing high enough to
miss that squall. If we're struck by lightning . . .'' He left it
dangling.

Dr. Lilly's face underwent a change of expression. As he
spun and sprinted toward the chain locker Joe noted that the
security expert had no difficulty in pronouncing an *sh*. There
was a sudden draft through the galley. Lilly had forced open
the forward hatch and was frantically passing waterproofed
cartons up on deck.

"Need any help?'' Joe called.

Dr. Lilly was too busy to reply.

There was a sudden growl-grind of electric motors as
Gorson punched roller reefing buttons and took in sail. The
sound ceased and the chief came below. "Any minute,'' he
said. "I tried to warn him but that gun nut's still deepsixing
boxes over the bow.''

Joe's amusement was tempered by the hope that Dr. Lilly
would finish before lightning struck.

Dr. Greybull finished stashing the apparatus that bore
some vestigial resemblance to the worm that Gorson and
Cook had set up inside a bell jar in an effor to produce a more
potent and less lethal raisin jack with vacuum distillation.
"Wonder if Lilly's saving anything.'' Dr. Greybull said.
"Do you have any conventional weapons that won't go off
unexpectedly from electrical transients?''

Joe had a navy issue .38 revolver.

"Couple of M-16s in the lazarette," Gorson volunteered.
"Is he throwing all the good stuff overboard?"

Joe nodded.

"Should've known some damned expert would screw it up," Gorson growled.

"Oh oh!" Cook muttered.

Joe felt his hair trying to stand away from his scalp—felt every follicle on his body twitch and tingle as the electrical charge built. Before he had time to become truly frightened the air about the ketch expanded, imploded, and he was deaf again, reeling from the concussion that seemed to reverberate not from a single explosion, but from a series of up-and-down alternations until the potential between clouds and sea had been equalized.

In the old days they had strung heavy cable from the backstay to the still and had depended on Freedy's scanning of the fathometer to achieve some kind of hit-or-miss resonance with the coil created by the still worm. Now Dr. Greybull had consolidated it all in a single suitcase-sized piece of gear. There was a muffled whump and the suitcase flew open. "I know I turned it off," Greybull muttered.

"I hope you brought some extra parts," Joe observed when the silence changed to a prolonged ringing in his ears. Shards and finely powdered glass littered the interior of the suitcase. The copper coil had melted into a shapeless lump.

"Don't worry." Dr. Greybull had the bedside manner of a highpriced general practitioner, though Greybull was not that kind of doctor. "We onloaded a couple of dozen spares several weeks ago."

Dr. Lilly's odd planes and angles of a face appeared at the forward end of the galley. Joe considered the doctor's slightly scorched air and was vaguely horrified at his own joy. "Can't imagine why nobody ever thought of electrical transients," Lilly said ruefully.

Because the people who did all the planning never did any time traveling, Joe thought. But he did not say it.

Lilly seemed shaken. Joe wondered if a few more moments of total terror could humanize this younger version of the Director. That, he suspected, was asking too much even of lightning. Lilly still stood at the head of the galley, obviously wanting to say something and not knowing how. "I'm not navy," he began. "Did mine in the army and the company."

By which Joe supposed he meant the CIA.

"Do they still say it the old way?"

Had a jolt of lightning permanently unhinged the security expert? "Say it any way you want to," Joe suggested.

Lilly's air was tentative. "Ship ahoy?"

Gorson and Joe charged for the cabin slide. Joe was the winner by a hand and foot.

The *Alice* rolled sickeningly in the short leftover chop of the squall. Joe stood in the kneedeep cockpit, bracing his back against the binnacle as he studied the horizon. The squall had blown mostly past them and the afternoon sun was obscured by clouds. Gorson fiddled with roller reefing, letting out the storm tris'l to absorb some of the snap of the ketch's vigorous roll.

Joe twiddled his binoculars into focus. The ship was not a ship. It was a slightly oversized speedboat and was, Joe saw abruptly, the kind of antiquated junk some overpaid rock star would have piddled his money away on back before the Arabs did their number on oil. The blackhulled cabin cruiser had been idling along on a NE heading. Abruptly it turned toward the *Alice*.

"Lost," Gorson predicted. "Running out of gas, and going to bug us for a tow. As if we were the frigging Coast Guard!"

As the blackhulled boat came closer a man on the flying bridge yelled something unintelligible. Still cursing those who go unprepared to sea, Gorson handed Joe the bullhorn.

"What's your problem?" Joe called.

The oilskin clad man on the other boat seemed startled. He yelled back and once more Joe couldn't hear. "Jesus Christ, a megaphone!" Gorson snarled. "Hasn't even got a bullhorn!"

Gorson had forgotten they were not in their own time. The distance closed and Joe raked the other boat with binoculars. There were several men and even, he thought, a woman. The man on the flying bridge was bulky as Gorson, and wore oilskins with the sleeves pushed up past his elbows.

"Where the hell you been?" the stranger called.

Joe and Gorson stared at each other.

"Laying off here damn near a week waiting for you," the man in oilskins called. "Your boss got some other supplier or what the hell . . ?"

"Supplier?" Joe echoed. "Supply what?"

"Booze. You ready to take it on or not?"

"Great!" Gorson had finally realized when they were. "Keep cool with Coolidge," he grunted.

Although Joe had once been an historian, he knew less about the early 20th century than he could toss off about Mycenean Greece or the sea raiders who had plagued Egypt's Middle Kingdom.

Men were drifting onto the *Alice's* deck to see what all the shouting was about. Abruptly the man in oilskins noted navy white hats and navy dungarees. "Twenty three skidoo!" he yelled. "God damned Coast Guard grabbed her."

Abruptly the black hulled vessel screamed on past the *Alice*. Twin, unmuffled Liberty engines, rocked the ketch in their wake. Joe faced Gorson. "Now we know how the original owner of the *Alice* kept his wine cellar stocked all through the long dry years."

There were three pop-whooshes in rapid succession. Joe spun and there was Lilly with his rapid fire launcher popping rockets after the disappearing rum runner. "I told you never to fire that thing aboard my ship again!" Joe roared. "Now give it to me."

"They're getting away!"

"They got away before you were hatched, you bornagain bastard!" Gorson contributed.

As Joe and Gorson converged on him Lilly's face turned dangerous. Then with a mercurial shift of attitude he smiled

and tossed the rocket launcher over the side. "Your ship,"
he said. "The ass that bleeds may be your own." Before
they could reply he turned and went below.

Joe sighed and turned to Dr. Greybull "It worked." he
conceded. "But the roaring twenties is still quite a jump from
the Council of Nicaea."

Greybull nodded. "I wish to holy Helmholtz that I could
understand this process. What I *suspect* is that we just happened to catch a weak stroke of lightning."

"Or forgot to cross your fingers."

"There is that too." Greybull took Joe seriously.

Joe took the makeshift tiller while Gorson devoted his
attention to roller reefing controls. Within a minute the *Alice*
was sluicing along under jib and storm tris'l.

Rose came on deck and surveyed the shattered mizzen. "I
can cut it off and restep it," he said. "It'd balance the push
even if we do have to tie in a reef."

Joe nodded. Where would he find timber for a new mizzen
mast along the barren coast of Baja? Gorson was putting
Hennis to the helm and giving him the course when Joe went
below to see what all the racket in the galley was about.

Dr. Greybull was not neither smiling nor tolerant. Lilly
stood, head drooping like a mule in a hailstorm, clenching
fists but not replying as Greybull stormed, "*Six* years in
Army Intelligence, *eight* years with the CIA, and you can't
read English? You were supposed to throw the *explosives*
overboard. Nobody told you to throw away every spare drive
tube for the time machine!"

Chapter 6

Joe stared, managing to conceal his joy at a legitimate reason to abort this mission while actually feeling sorry for the fanatical security expert. "All right," he told Lilly. "Don't go marching off the fantail. We'll work something out."

"What?" Cook asked. "Last time we had enough stuff aboard to build a dozen stills. Ran out of bell jars and we cut the bottoms off distilled water jugs."

Joe's joy ceased. "Don't we have any bottles aboard?"

The planes and angles of Lilly's narrowskulled face shifted to a tentative optimism. "A couple of quarts of Wild Turkey," he admitted.

"Too small," Cook said. "And there ain't ary an inch of copper tubing. The water lines are all plastic."

"He's right," Abe Rose contributed. "They took out the diesel and put in an electric and all those batteries and solar collectors. We got miles of bus bar but no fuel lines—" Abruptly the engineman paused. "After all, it's an electrical coil we're trying to make—not a still. Suppose it makes any difference?''

It would make a difference to their auxiliary engine, to the fathometer, the radar, the electric galley stove, the lights, the electric winches and what remained of their roller reefing gear. Joe knew he should have refused flatly to move backward in time aboard any ship that could not be worked by time honored methods—with hard fists and hemp. Too late now.

"Only sixty years from home," Gorson growled.

Freedy removed thick lensed glasses and rubbed his nose. "Know how to walk it?" he asked.

"Last time at least we had some broads to break the monotony," Gorson groused.

Joe could have done all day without that reminder. He felt his stomach churn again.

Dr. Greybull's fury with the multiple thumbed security man had abated. "You uh—" He faced Gorson and Cook. "You did the original research, cobbled up the first device out of odds and ends. I've read the reports, studied the photos, and there are times when I almost think I understand it." He paused again and passed his hand through abundant gray hair. Turning to Rose, he added, "With all the solar collectors and batteries and electric drives aboard, surely there must be a few spare feet of copper cable."

Rose agreed that this was probable. "But it won't do us any good without glass."

"Too bad we didn't accept," Greybull muttered.

"Accept what?" Joe demanded.

"A short time ago a stranger was offering to transfer a load of goods. No doubt most of them were packaged in glass."

Son of a bitch! Then Joe remembered the speed with which those Libery engines had departed. "Never catch him."

"Bull!" Dr. Lilly was returning to his normal obnoxious self. "I don't claim to be the world's best marksman," he said, "but right now they're patching up the hole where at least one of those heat-seekers went up a hot exhaust pipe."

Joe turned but Freedy was ahead of him. Thicklensed glasses back in place, the radioman was firing up the radar. "There's a blip about five miles off on 85° true," he said.

Gorson was tearing up through the cabin slide to order a course change.

The squall was long gone and no others in sight. The wind had shifted around to the normal westerly trades pattern. Joe went below again and studied the radar. Convinced that the weather held no surprises for several hours, he ordered the storm tris'l unbent and replaced by the main.

Fifteen minutes later the jib had also been replaced by the jenny and the *Alice* was hissing through a gentle ground swell, taking occasional dollops of brine over her lee rail, and sailing nicely without the mizzen on this point of wind. Abruptly Joe saw partial solutions to two problems—and that he still had one problem unresolved. "Dr. Lilly!"

"Sir!" The security expert erupted smartly from the cabin slide and faced Joe in the kneedeep cockpit.

"Since you threw the wrong thing overboard, may we assume the explosives remain intact?"

The planes and angles of the security man's face shifted as he realized he had screwed up again. "I'll get right on it, sir."

"Not yet," Joe said. "For the time being we won't be looking for any more lightning. This may be the beginning of a long hard winter."

Lilly studied Joe for an instant, then abruptly saluted. Joe wondered if it was mockery or if the security man had simply forgotten he was now a civilian.

Abe Rose had dragooned the three new boys into opening every hatch and locker aboard the *Alice* as he inventoried stores and tried to learn just where in Himmler's whimsy the electrical spares, if any, had been stashed.

Joe studied the sails for flutter. Howard Hennis, though probably from a non-yachting background, had a feel for the wind. The black was sailing the ketch on her best point, using every tiny shift of the brisk trade to run slantwise over the ground swell, as he held the *Alice* in a constant precarious balance with her lee rail only inches from awash. Joe nodded and went below.

Assuming the blackhulled rum runner did not finish repairs and start moving again, it would take at least 40 minutes. But why worry? The Coolidge era skipper would never have dreamed of radar. Abruptly Joe remembered Ma Trimble. Whatever had happened to that timewarped speakeasy proprietor in this law-and-order age of police spies? Joe had lost track of them all during the years of stonewalling.

He found himself up forward looking into the chain locker. It was unchanged from the last time he had sailed this ship: a crawl hole through from the fo'c's'l, a deck eye through which the anchor chain passed, and a hundred fathoms of hot-stretch nylon rope to extend the anchor chain for the near-bottomless places they used to anchor off the continental shelf. The chain locker was still there. The girl who had curtained off the crawl hole and used to sleep there was not. He would never see Raquel again.

What was wrong with him? Why couldn't he pull his life together and forget a girl he had only known a few weeks, a girl from some 10th century Spanish village who would have been totally out of her depth in any modern world? Joe had been passed over for promotion. It was not all the navy's fault.

He had wanted to stay in the past, in some back corner of the Alhambra performing his annual miracle—some tiny improvement in weaponry to keep some Moorish king happy and keep Joe and his people wellfed. But he *had* come back—to witness the growth of the Imperial Presidency.

It was not a perfect world but law-and-order seemed preferable to the chaotic alternatives for which the wildeyed shouted. If Joe could just not let his contempt be so obvious. Small wonder that he had not progressed in the navy. So she was gone. He tried to shake off the rage that threatened to leak out of his eyes.

They were heading for the blackhulled boat. No hope of

peacable commerce after Lilly's tactics. But Joe had faced his share of violence. He would board them, take whatever five gallon jars they had, and leave the wretches congratulating themselves that they were not in irons and being towed back to San Diego. It could be worse, Joe reminded himself. To kill them or sink their boat might have repercussions in the time stream. He tore himself from the chain locker's painful memories and went looking for Lilly.

The security expert sat at one of the settee bunks by the galley table. "How are you fixed for small arms?" Joe asked.

"Classified," Lilly said.

"The beast of burden that bleeds," Joe quoted Lilly, "will not be mine. Issue weapons to my people or once we overtake those rum runners you can board them alone."

"That's what I'm sworn and paid to do." Lilly was unemotional.

Joe had heard fantastic stories about the Director's penchant for holding his hands over burning candles. Birds of a feather, he supposed. "Think you can handle it?" he asked.

Lilly shrugged.

"In case you can't," Joe said, "I want small arms issued to everyone aboard."

"To rescue me?" Lilly's tone was mocking.

"To hell with you and the Director and the whole goddam Imperial Presidency! You want to get blown away that's your trip. Mine is to keep my ship and my people intact."

"That clears the air quite nicely." Lilly gave a mocking salute and left the galley. When Joe went on deck a few minutes later the security expert was handing out M-16s and making sure everyone knew how to change a clip and charge the chamber. "And don't go firing full automatic," he was saying. "It just wastes ammunition of a calibre they didn't manufacture during the Coolidge administration."

Abe Rose accepted his weapon with a snarled "Of course I know how it works. Why do you think I deepsixed mine for a Kalashnikov the first time I went upriver?" He went back to opening hatches, rummaging through carefully and compactly stored supplies, cursing the ingenuity that could crowd all this gear into an 89 foot ketch and then forget to supply a manifest to tell where everything was. "The lazarette," he growled. "We've been everywhere else."

It was taking Rose forever to search the ship precisely because supplies were laid in so compactly. Each compartment had to be emptied, and then repacked in the same exact order before moving on to the next, lest the *Alice's* fiberglassed and solar panelled decks be buried under mounds that could wash overboard the first time the steersman's attention wandered.

Joe consulted his watch. The rum runner had only been five miles alee, according to the radar. He studied the sea ahead with binoculars. Belowdecks Freedy hunched over the radar. "Still four miles," he said. "Moving a little slower than we are, and she hadn't changed course."

So the bootleggers were not totally disabled in spite of Lilly's heatseeking rockets.

"Well how 'bout that!" Rose was standing at the edge of the lazarette hatch cover looking down. Joe guessed he had finally found the copper cable.

Gorson approached the stern and looked down into the lazarette, which reminded Joe that the bos'n and the cook had once hidden surplus weapons there to finance their own little war. "God damn!" Gorson was saying. "Looks like it might turn into a fun trip after all!"

This was not a proper reaction to copper cable. Joe stepped up out of the kneedeep cockpit and strode aft to gaze down into the lazarette. Hollowed out of carefully stowed supplies was a small and barely habitable bunk. The bunk was inhabited. Blonde hair was uncombed but Joe knew at once who it had to be. He had stared across his office often enough to know those endless legs could only belong to Yeoperson Margaret White.

Dr. Lilly came aft. "Am I interrupting anyting?" he asked. It was the first time Joe had seen him smile. Joe decided he preferred Dr. Lilly when he was not smiling.

Chapter 7

Yeoperson Margaret White looked up at Joe. "Sorry, sir," she said. "There just wasn't any other place to run." She wore a white uniform-of-the-day blouse. A trim tailored navy blue skirt extended to the middle of a kneecap that bore no visible defects. Her uniform had several. The blouse was ripped and buttons were missing. Her torn skirt offered startling flashes of pantyhose as she climbed stiffly from the lazarette.

"What happened?" Joe demanded. Even as he said it he knew.

"I was fair game," she said. "from the instant when everyone suddenly knew you'd been sent off someplace you wouldn't be coming back from. You might have told me—at least said good bye."

Joe felt something die inside him. He had never felt capable of loving this able woman but he had *liked* her. Margaret White had not volunteered to be blonde or more than usually attractive. She tried to live quietly and men would not let her. He remembered when such chauvinism would have elicited tar and feathers from an outraged citizenry. These days people were more concerned with their own affairs.

All hands were staring. Joe ignored them as he led the girl below, into his cabin. "Did they . . ?"

Margaret was not a girl who required elaborate explanations. "One lived," she said. "I altered his hormonal balance with my knee."

"One lived? You killed somebody?"

"The base security officer."

"My God, what happened?"

She shrugged. "Drunk. Or smoking something funny soaked in something funnier."

"And I suppose it's your word and no witnesses?" The base security officer had been chief thug in the plot to nail Joe's yeoperson for lesbianism.

"A girl who doesn't melt into a mush of hopeless passion at the sight of a fifty year old redneck is obviously a sexual deviate." Margaret White did not sound bitter. She was merely stating facts in a brittle, précise voice.

Once Joe would have been outraged by this recital. But he had seen too many outrages. What on earth was he going to do with her? Being selfish, he knew. But he was also being captain. There were urgent matters pending. "Uh, look," he said, "Help yourself in my locker. They won't fit very well but you'd better get into dungarees or something. And don't leave this cabin till I come back." He tried not to look at the endless expanse of leg that emerged from her ruined skirt.

Now that she had achieved relative safety, his yeoperson's brittle reserve was reaching its limits. Joe gave her a quick pat on the shoulder and closed the door on sudden explosive weeping.

On deck the blackhulled rum runner seemed forgotten.

"Acts like she knows you." Gorson's grin was wolfish.

"My yeoperson." Joe was remembering all the hell women had caused the last time he commanded the *Alice*.

Dr. Lilly forced his way between them. "Who's the broad?"

"She's a clean-living yeoperson who just killed the security officer who tried to rape her," Joe snapped.

"Good for her!" Cook cackled, then sobered. "Goldang, Mr. Rate, how we ever gonna take her back home?"

Gorson's grin widened. "You recommending her for the good conduct medal?"

Lilly gave Joe the fishy look of a man who knows he's being lied to. "When the Russians take over you'll remember me as part of the good old days," he reminded.

"Think I see 'em," Cook said.

"The Russians?"

"That overgrowed speed boat," Cook said.

Lilly's face shifted into hard awareness. "Sure you don't want me to use a rocket launcher?" His attitude was mocking.

"Couldn't the administration's quarrel with the American citizenry at least be a limited war?" Joe asked. "Those people over there could be our immediate ancestors."

The *Alice* was hissing along at a good six, moving up on a blackhulled boat that seemed barely to be making steerageway. Joe fiddled with binoculars that somebody nearsighted or perverse twisted out of focus every time he put them down.

In spite of Lilly's claims about his heatseeking rockets, the blackhulled boat seemed undamaged. Somebody had banged the binoculars far enough out of collimation to produce a slight double image. Joe closed one eye and studied the transom stern for signs of repair. Black paint seemed slightly newer than on the rum runner's sides but he saw no evidence of damage. Joe could not put his finger on it but he knew something was different.

"Mexican flag," Lilly observed.

Joe shrugged. Any smuggler would have a full complement of flags and documentation to back them up. But this had to be the same boat they had hailed less than an hour ago. Even in this roaring twenties era of rakish, narrow beamed wooden hulls there was slight chance of that much coincidence.

Uniformed crew lounged on the foredeck. From the flying bridge binoculars glinted as someone returned Joe's compliment but this time the smugglers were not running. Abruptly Joe saw what else was different. The blackhulled boat had a swivel mounted one-pounder on the bow and another atop the high transom stern. He could not imagine how he had missed seeing it the first time. The more he thought about it the surer Joe was that those guns had not been there an hour ago.

Neither gun was manned. The rum runners viewed the *Alice's* approach with a calm that caused a stir on the back of Joe's neck. The twenties had been awash in the antique but still lethal armaments of World War One. If they were not manning the one-pounders then what other surprise awaited him?

Squinting through out-of-collimation binoculars, he searched for the man who had worn oilskins an hour ago. He decided he was just not recognizing the stocky figure in different clothing. The crewmen were dark, Indian looking.

Gorson took the wheel as the *Alice* began to draw alongside. "That electric engine ready?" he asked.

Rose nodded and stopped puttering with the shattered mizzen mast.

Gorson took in sail until the ketch matched speed, running with the weather gage on the idling black hull's starboard side. As men put out fenders Joe noted that those aboard the other boat were all Mexicans.

They had panicked and yelled in fluent American an hour ago. A short, dark man in naval uniform with three narrow stripes round his sleeves stared down at Joe. "*¿Que hubo?*" he demanded, then switched to heavily accented English. "You have trobble?"

It was the same boat but it was not the same people. Abruptly Joe knew what had happened. "Cool it," he growled.

The *Alice's* people stood looking embarrassedly at the M-16's Lilly had issued. They began stowing them. Turning back to the man on the flying bridge Joe began,

"Necesitamos agua," then decided he might as well tell the truth.

It wasn't water the *Alice* needed. What might save them was some of the 5-gallon glass bottles in which potable varieties of this beverage used to be sold. But would *aguadores* have used those bottles three generations ago? Joe was sorting through long unused Spanish for the proper words when abruptly Dr. Lilly took a running leap over the *Alice's* rail and landed in a menacing crouch, rocket launcher and all, on the rum runner's deck.

"Geronimo!" the security expert yelled.

Joe stared, his mouth open with unadulterated horror. "Come back here you crazy son of a bitch!" he yelled.

"¡Cabron!" a deckhand on the blackhulled boat added, and wrapped a boat hook around the planes and angles of Dr. Lilly's ascetic head.

Joe knew it was his own fault. But how could he have expected even a madman to take him seriously about assaulting a ship singlehanded? In the nightmare instant while Joe refused to believe this was really happening he found time to wonder how many more rocket launchers the security expert would toss over the side before he ran out of them. He would never get a chance now. Not even Dr. Lilly's head could be as hard as a boat hook.

"¡Está loco!" Joe yelled, and made corkscrew motions to the side of his head, then turned to yell at his own people once more to cool it. Weapons forgotten, they stared aghast. Lilly lay motionless on the deck of the blackhulled yacht.

Joe raised his hands, waved his arms, yelled placating nonsense and strove mightily to circumvent the logical conclusion to Lilly's rashness. The rest of his people saw what had not been apparant to the security expert, that these were not the same people who had cut and run an hour ago. They also saw that there were about three times as many of them as were aboard the *Alice*.

Run for it and Joe knew this time he would lose. Under full sail and power the *Alice* could do eight. The rum runner had streaked past him at thirty-five. He could not bring himself to attack the navy of a nation presumably at peace with his own. Still pantomiming innocence and struggling to disown the insane Dr. Lilly, he saw outraged Mexicans pour on deck, pour over the rail. Half of Joe's remaining seven men were unsure how to charge an M-16. Rose knew the weapon well enough to discard it for a Stillson wrench.

Witnessing the free-for-all on the *Alice's* crowded deck Joe was reminded that, no matter what he had occasionally done under duress, he was not cut out for combat. Damn Lilly! Triggerhappy superpatriot had gotten them into the wrong war in the wrong place *at the wrong time*.

"¡*Espérense!*" he yelled, but the Mexicans were not waiting. Brown sailors poured from the bowels of the rum runner. Somebody got off a brief burst from an M-16 but Joe saw no evidence that anyone had been hit. The Mexicans charged with the blind fury of the peaceloving who've been attacked once again by a powerful and treacherous neighbor. These men, Joe realized, would have fresh memories of General Pershing, when an illiterate bandit had led the United States Army on a fourteen month wild goose chase. Villa's bloodless outmaneuvering of the Punitive Expedition had been more comic, but no less humiliating than Vietnam. These men would be delighted at this opportunity to do it again.

Kraus, was yelling something in Spanish. It did not sound one half so placating as the things Joe was trying to say. The new boy's voice rang through the din and Joe heard a suggestion that would have aborted Oedipus.

Hennis had dropped into a fighting crouch and was moving with surprising deftness for so gangling a man. Short Mexican sailors struggled to climb over the the ring of victims that began to surround the black.

A huge Indian advanced on Joe, grinning as he flexed his biceps. Behind him Joe saw Gorson and Cook go down under a swarm of smaller men. Since the Mexicans gave his gray hair and beard their due respect, Dr. Greybull was out of it. A couple of sailors were binding the scientist's hands behind him. "¡*Paz!*" Joe yelled.

Uninterested in peace, the Indian grinned and swung a hamsized fist.

Joe ducked inside the roundhouse swing and gave the huge man a punch to solar plexus. He was backing off to follow up with one in the chops when abruptly Joe realized:

1.   The binoculars still hung around his neck by a strap that the Indian was pulling and,

2.   The Indian was still grinning as he began twisting the leather strap.

What am I doing here? Joe asked himself. *I'm too old for this. My best shot and he doesn't even . . . If I'm not careful I might get this guy mad at me!*

Joe's vision narrowed, then turned into the dotflecks of an untuned TV. Joe knew he should have acted decisively. Was there any way he could square things with the Mexican commander? No matter whose fault, the navy was going to tie the can on Joe for this disaster. The hell of it was, Joe knew it really *was* his fault. Once beyond swimming distance of San Diego the first thing he should have done was to throw that psychopathic security expert overboard! Irrelevantly, he found himself wondering what would happen to his yeoperson. Margaret White was nowhere in sight.

Joe struggled to focus on the face that loomed over him. The binocular strap loosened for an instant and he caught a breath. The Indian was grinning. Joe compressed his chest down over gulped air like a mountain climber and as his vision momentarily cleared he drove the stiff fingers of one hand into the Indian's grinning face. He spiked his other hand into the solar plexus. The Indian still grinned but he no longer twisted the binocular strap.

Joe got his feet against the huge man's chest and propelled himself away from reaching hamsized fists. He struggled to his feet and turned to look squarely down the bore of a carbine. The barrel was short but the hole was wide. Joe raised his hands.

Chapter 8

"What you do here?" the Mexican commander demanded.

Joe stood before the desk-chart table flanked by short sailors who trained Colt .45's on him. Once he had been fluent in Spanish. He felt a twinge at the memory of how he had acquired his fluency. Struggling to recall the words, he began, *"Soy capitán de corveta de la Marina de los Estados Unidos."*

"¿De veras?" The Mexican's tone was scathing.

"I kept trying to tell you he was insane." Joe was referring to Dr. Lilly.

"Obviously," the Mexican said. "Not even a crazy gringo attacks a warship all by himself."

"We'll lock him up where he can do no harm," Joe promised. "If he's still alive, that is. And we'll compensate for any damages." Even if he could get in touch with his government, would they agree?

"Undoubtedly." The Mexican was short and dark, with the dyspeptic air of a man who spends too much of his time listening to lies. "Now tell me who you really are."

"United States Navy—" Joe began.

"¡Basta!" the Mexican roared. "I'm paid to listen to smugglers lie. My pay is not sufficient to swallow insults."

"But we are—"

"Gringos whose crudely counterfeited money is printed on paper several centimeters too small? Gringos whose uniform is not that worn by gringo Navy? Gringos with too many stars on your flag?"

Joe suspected any explanation offered would be deemed insufficient. "All right!" he snapped. "We're time travelers."

"All travel in Mexico is temporal," the Mexican commander said. "Religion has been outlawed since the revolution."

"Not that kind of temporal," Joe struggled. "Viajeros temporales. We come back from the future when uniforms and flags have changed—when Alaska and Hawaii have become states."

The Mexican was amused. "And my country too, no doubt, is now a state or at least a colony."

"Part of your populace wishes it were. But actually, there are so many of you in the States now that Spanish is an official second language."

"Gringos are finally living up to the treaty of Guadalupe Hidalgo?"

"The border is not open but more of yours come north than ours go south. Nothing stops them."

"Why would anyone wish to leave Mexico?"

Joe sighed. "And I insult your intelligence? In your—this day there are 14 million in the whole country and you import food. In my time there are 12 million mouths in your capital city alone."

The captain emitted an incredulous bark of laughter.

The door behind Joe opened. "Con la novedad, mi capitán." The sailor continued his report in Spanish too fast for Joe to follow. The captain surveyed Joe with cold eyes. As the report continued the tiny spark of sympathy in those eyes screwed down to a vanishing point six decimal places to the left of a New England banker.

"United States Navy," he sneered. "A *woman* aboard a *sailing ship!* Enough *simplezas.*" He gestured and the short sailors with pistols nudged Joe out of the cabin.

As he was prodded back on deck Joe could not imagine where all his people had been taken. What was happening to poor Margaret now? Sailors guided him forward and down another ladder and Joe discovered that most of the forward section consisted of small cabins. At some period in its career this vessel had carried passengers. He remembered that coastwise shipping had still been competitive with rails in the twenties.

The aftermost cabin had undergone another conversion. As its barred metal door slammed behind him Joe saw where his crew was. Dr. Lilly stretched full length on the upper of two bunks, breathing with noisy regularity. Joe's relief was mixed with annoyance.

Howard Hennis's feet hung out of the end of the lower bunk. Someone had folded a jumper and put it beneath the black's swollen, lumpy head. The rest of the *Alice's* people sat on the deck nursing assorted bruises. There was no sign of Margaret White.

"Howdy, Mr. Rate," Cook greeted. "You think they'll let us go?"

"If you think that you'll think they really believe we're time travelers."

"You told them?" Dr. Greybull was shocked.

"No danger of anybody believing us."

"But what if they did? Just imagine for example what could happen in the stock market if one man had tomorrow's newspaper! We could come back to a world in which Mexico is the superpower."

"I believe I mentioned some such possibility at that conference in Washington," Joe snapped.

"That's different," Dr. Greybull protested. "All parameters for the Council at Nicaea have been computed to the ultimate—"

"Not to me," Gorson growled. "Just what're we supposed to do there?"

"Don't worry," Cook said with a glance at the guard outside the barred door. "Ain't no way we ever gonna do it."

It was the single bright side that Joe could see in their present situation.

"We must complete our original mission," Greybull rubbed at red welts on his wrists where the rope had bitten in. "Time is not on our side."

"Never has been," Gorson muttered.

Kraus, the latino boy, looked disbelievingly from face to face. He shook his head and stepped over legs toward the barred door where he tried to strike up a conversation with the guard.

"Things went wrong," Greybull explained. "The Russians emerged from their Arctic cocoon and are busy driving a wedge between the western and Arab worlds. We can bomb each other to extermination or we can go back and remove the cause. I leave it to you which course is the more humane."

"Mister Rate," Cook asked. "What's he talkin' about?"

"The Council of Nicaea had something to do with the Arian Heresy," Joe said. "Been a while since I took any interest in history so I'd probably get it all wrong. But the geniuses have computed it to the last infinitesimal."

"What are *you* talking about?" Gorson demanded.

"Oh my God!" It was Hennis. The gangling black straightened painfully and sat on the edge of the bunk holding his head. "You fixing to blow some holes in the Athanasian Creed?"

Joe's eyes widened. All hands turned to stare at the black.

"Homoousios and all that 'don't matter one iota' crap," Hennis continued. "All those old dudes poking each other's eyes out over how to spell a word—as if it made any difference."

"But it does," Greybull protested.

"I didn't join the navy to fight no religious war," Hennis said. "I'm a muslim."

"Is that anything like a baptist?" Cook asked.

"You'd be amazed at the similarities," Abe Rose growled.

"We aren't being sent there for religious reasons," Joe said. "The theory is that the wrong side won."

"That's religion."

"That's economics," Greybull said. "The clash began when Christianity supplanted the older polytheistic religions."

"Polly who?" Cook demanded.

"People in western Europe had a god for wood, one for water, one for everything," Joe explained. "They turned Christianity into the same mishmosh with their saints and father, son, holy-ghost divisions. The easterners, having already invented algebra, couldn't accept the math in $3 = 1$."

"Voodoo works that way—oh Jesus!" Hennis nursed his head. "The Christian god's too busy. For a little problem they don't run to the big man. Just kill a chicken for the neighborhood spook."

"Which heathen practice makes the distraught missionary pray to his saint for guidance." Abe Rose emitted no hint of smile.

The guard at the door handed his pistol to a taller man and departed. Joe saw with a sense of forboding that the new guard was the huge Indian who had strangled him.

"Ain't fightin' no religious wars," Cook said.

"Not as long as we're in here anyway," Rose added.

"It's not religion," Joe snapped. "This whole insane operation is for oil."

"We gonna drill for it?" Gorson demanded. "How do we get it back?"

"The idea is that if the Christians hadn't insulted the eastern peoples with the trinity there would never have been any Islam. Moslem theology stems from the Jewish concept of a single god. If the Council had voted the other way the west and the Arabs would share a common culture and religion and Mohammed might have been Bishop of Medina. The Russians would be off in happy Arctic isolation firing their boilers with yak chips."

"Whooee," Cook wheezed. "You really think that'd work?"

"Does anything? If the experts calculated down to the last infinitesimal then why did they send along a weapons expert and compute us into a Mexican brig?"

"Is that crazy SOB still alive?" Gorson asked.

"I am," Lilly said from the top bunk. "And if any of you are religious, then pray these Mexicans never learn who we really are."

"Tu" The huge Indian at the door was beckoning to Joe. *"Ven aquí."*

Acutely aware of the red welt around his neck, Joe approached the barred door. The Indian opened it and prodded him up a ladder, then aft. They stood on deck, the Indian grinning at Joe, at the sea, and at the mass of short dark sailors who swarmed over the *Alice*. Several minutes passed and then Margaret White emerged from the captain's cabin between two sailors. She seemed smaller and totally defenseless in Joe's too-big dungarees. "I told nothing," she said as they whisked her past. The Indian pushed Joe into the cabin.

"Conque siempre sí son viajeros temporales," the captain said.

"Sorry about that," Joe lied. "No, we're really not time travelers at all."

"¿Verdad?" I always knew gringos were intelligent. Not only do all your men have books but they all read in English." The captain's air was mocking.

"And you do not?" Joe hoped.

"With difficulty. But numbers are the same in any language." The captain rummaged through books that littered his desk. "I find it hard to believe in time travel. Even harder is to explain why every book and periodical aboard your ship is dated at least 50 years in the future, along with the coins in every pocket. And would even gringos print nautical almanacs with positions that the stars will not occupy for another half century?"

"Veritas filia temporis" Joe muttered.

"You are also a priest? What did you say?"

"Truth is the daughter of time."

The Mexican smiled. "You are no priest. You are an even better catch."

"I beg your pardon?"

"You know old languages." The Mexican smiled. "Therefore you study history."

Joe knew he was not going to like what came next. "Ancient history," he hastened. "Whatever you want to know about the Greeks or the Romans—anything up to the age of the Vikings. But I know next to nothing about the history of your era. It was too close to be considered history when I went to school." He glanced at his wrist where there had been a watch. "We're on a tight schedule," he said. "And this mission is important. It concerns the future of the entire world."

"My concerns," the captain said, "Are my country and myself." He held up Joe's digital watch. "I can understand this," he said. "But could you explain this?" He was holding up the pocket navigational calculator.

"It could damage the fabric of time merely for you to know about those things. If you could just return our property and let us get on our way—"

"Time," the captain mused. "Don't worry. I'm sure you'll know something useful."

"It's dangerous," Joe protested.

"Not to me. Any tinkering here will only damage your future." He gave Joe a thin smile. "Would you throw away tomorrow's newspaper?" Then abruptly the Mexican's face changed. "Yes! you would."

"I beg your pardon?" Joe said.

"You travel in time. For you there is no wondering about what the future holds."

"I'm afraid it doesn't work that well," Joe said. "We have nothing but trouble with it."

"Ah?"

"It's not working right at all."

"I was afraid," the Mexican captain said thoughtfully, "That it might be something back in your own time— something beyond your control."

Joe realized abruptly that he was coming down with a terminal case of foot-in-mouth disease.

"You have a time machine," the Mexican said. "Where is it?"

Chapter 9

The captain began offering blustery scenarios of all the unpleasant ends to which Joe and his people could come.

"*¡Basta!*" Joe finally said. "As you remarked some time ago, that's enough."

The captain was half out of his chair and guards were cocking pistols as Joe continued: "Why don't you stuff your *machismo* where it belongs and devote thirty seconds to thinking?"

"The man with the gun does not have to think."

"Nor does the man with time on his side." Joe paused to let this sink in and to improvise his next shot. "You have radio. Do you suppose another sixty years of invention has not produced arms beyond your dreams *and constant communication with my government*?" Joe made a weary gesture. "Some of those books you seized may mention how, a generation ago, we destroyed cities with a single bomb. Search your soul and your history for some hint that my prince does not value my ship and my people more than the cinder that will be your *patria*."

As he said it Joe was sickened by the knowledge that he

was coming more and more to Dr. Lilly's way of thinking. But if he didn't terrorize this captain out of his blind greed . . . "May I know your name?"

"Why does my name interest you?" the Mexican barked.

"History recalls the name of Antonio López de Santa Anna, whose only sin was to bankrupt Mexico and lose half its territory. For a country and a people to disappear without knowing which fool destroyed them seems unfitting." Joe paused, giving time for this to penetrate the captain and the sailors who guarded him.

"I and my people will escape, of course," he added with an airiness he wished he could feel. Was any of this getting through to the expressionless guards? Joe saw the captain's indecision. He didn't believe it but neither had he believed in time travel until the evidence became overwhelming.

"You survive death then?"

Abruptly Joe saw the corner into which he had painted himself. The captain had discovered a foolproof method of verifying Joe's boast. He was drawing his pistol.

Joe stared into a hole that seemed much larger than forty five hundredths of an inch. He took a deep breath. "No," he said. "We die like anyone else. But do not forget the time machine."

"Ah?" The captain could not see the connection.

Having never tried it, neither could Joe. He did not, however, feel that this situation demanded a strict adherence to the truth. *"Procura no ser pendejo,"* Joe said. The plea not to be stupid was directed to himself as much as to the livid captain whose finger whitened on the trigger.

"Dying," Joe continued, "is painful. So painful that the memory reverberates both ways, into future and past."

The muzzle of the captain's pistol wavered. "Explain."

"Our friends have all the time in several worlds. It's simple to trace the events that led to a friend's death—and then alter those events." Joe smiled into the pistol bore.

"But a man who has been killed remembers the pain even after his friends alter history to prevent his death. The man who has been murdered may enliven dull afternoons by reviving his murderer. A murdered man devises ingenious methods of prolonging pain. *He has the time.*"

Joe saw that he had everyone's full attention. One corner of his mind asked if it could actually work—assuming they had a time machine that worked and could be controlled to pinpoint a moment. *A moment when Raquel . . .*

He forced himself into a bantering, professorial attitude and continued lecturing. "A belief in law and order once prevailed in the English speaking countries—to such an extent that the concept of private justice almost disappeared.

"Now you and I," he continued, "know the law is a joke on the poor, that any murder can be fixed for a week's pay. The deterrent is not the law. What gives assassins second thoughts is the knowledge that victims have families to avenge them. Yet you cope only with friends and relations—not with the victim."

Joe paused and looked around at his openmouthed guards, then back at the pistol in the captain's hand. The captain seemed to have forgotten it. Joe took another breath and continued, "A murdered man does not laugh it off. *Me la vas a pagar, cabrón.*" Joe stared unsmiling into the captain's eyes and repeated the insult. "You'll pay your debt to me, *wife-peddler.*"

As the captain aimed his pistol again. Joe suspected he had overdone it. But to back off now would kill him just as surely as to charge ahead. Joe inventoried hidden assets and dredged up another smile. "Unless your mother, wife, sister and daughter pay me first," he added.

There was a convulsive movement but the captain lowered the pistol. He sat rigid, staring at Joe for a long moment. "*Llévenselo*" he finally grunted.

As the sailors herded him back down to the brig Joe sensed that at this stage he could sell them any kind of nonsense. What lies could be more terrifying than H-bombs? He had another sudden thought. "This boat," he said. "American smugglers once owned it. Did it come limping into some Mexican port with a big hole in its stern?"

The shorter of the sailors studied Joe with some surprise.

"You do not know of the things that filled every newspaper when our government seized this boat?"

It had never happened in Joe's past. Not unless he and Dr. Lilly and those heatseeking rockets were locked into an endless loop. "We've been away for a while," he explained. "How long ago did it happen?"

The sailor shrugged. "Two—three months."

So there had been another time jump between Lilly's rocketry a few hours ago and now . . .

Dr. Greybull was hobbling up the ladder, a single sailor behind him. The shorter sailor switched his attention to the scientist, leaving Joe in charge of the huge man who had choked him. "¿Eres gringo?" the Indian asked.

Joe regarded him in surprise. "Aren't you Mexican?" he asked. "Of course I'm an American."

The sailor spat, not even trying for the rail. "You really are gringo?" he repeated.

"I'm an officer in the United States Navy."

"You kill Mexicans?"

"We haven't been at war for over a hundred years." Joe had momentarily forgotten Veracruz and the Pershing Expedition.

The huge sailor wore the same grin as when he had been twisting the binocular straps. Without comment he put Joe back in the brig.

"What happened?" Gorson asked.

"I'm not sure."

"We'll need every bit of information if we're going to plan our stragety." Lilly's eyes were turning black and the ear where the boat hook had connected stuck out at an odd angle.

"You're officially insane," Joe said. "Act normal and you'll convince them." Joe inventoried the crowded cell. Dr. Greybull was the only one missing. Joe wished he'd had time to get his story straight with the civilian scientist. Perhaps the captain's English would not be good enough to understand.

"We kill people," Joe began, and primed them all to back up his tall tale of posthumous vengeance. "Kraus, damn it, stop swapping lies with that guard and get over here with the rest of us.''

Even Dr. Lilly thought Joe's idea was brilliant. ''I bet it'll work too—once we get the bugs out of the machine. Damn! What a control!''

''Control?'' Joe echoed.

''Sentence a man to ten firing squads—or perhaps a shooting, a hanging, an electrocution and the gas chamber. Run a rebel through that two or three times and he ought to turn pretty lawabiding.''

There would always be others like the good doctor—but a man had to start somewhere. Joe understood for the first time that sooner or later he was going to have to kill Dr. Lilly. The door opened and the grinning Indian pushed Dr. Greybull in. He beckoned Gorson.

''What'd he ask you?'' Lilly demanded.

Dr. Greybull was showing his age and a growth of whiskers around the edges of his neatly trimmed beard. He gave the security man a look of annoyance and turned to Joe. ''Your counterpart doesn't understand English as well as he tries to speak it. I did nothing to make his job easier.''

''Did he ask about reviving the dead with time travel?''

''Is that what he was trying to get at?''

''What did you tell him?''

''Same spiel I give appropriations committees—pages of meaningless equations punctuated with occasional 'therefores' or 'obviouslys'. Neither congress nor the Mexican navy has ever heard of the emperor's new clothes.''

Joe regarded the old man with new respect.

''What's this about raising stiffs?'' Greybull asked. ''I can't even make the damned machine work.''

Joe left Dr. Lilly extolling the time machine's ability to control dissension. He turned from Greybull's growing horror and saw his latino crewman once more talking with the guard at the door. ''Kraus!'' Joe yelled.

The latino waved a shushing hand behind his back and continued in deep converse with a Mexican sailor. Joe supposed he ought to do something about restoring discipline.

But there was always the chance that the boy knew what he was doing.

"Are you of Mexican origin?" he asked when the guard had been relieved again and Kraus abandoned the door.

"No, sir. My parents were born in Mexico." Kraus's English was good enough when he worked at it but the language was obviously an afterthought in his curriculum.

"Whence came the Kraus?"

The young sailor shrugged. "Not all of Maximilian's soldiers made it home. My grandfather settled near Bacochibampo. That's in Sonora."

Joe had seen enough Yuto-aztecan place names to have some inkling of *bampo*. "Some kind of a waterhole, I suppose?"

Kraus's eyes widened and he spoke rapidly.

Joe did not understand but he knew these glottal stops and geminated vowels could not belong in any European language. "My god," he gasped. "Are you Yaqui?"

Kraus drew himself proudly to his full five-five. "I dance pascolas first time when I was fourteen."

"Welcome to the club," Abe Rose said sourly.

Kraus gave the engineman a questioning look.

"I'm also a member of one of those odd little groups who wrote their own contract with God," Rose said. "We've been bleeding over a piece of real estate several thousand years longer than you."

"In 1926 we took the president's train," Kraus said. "We don't turn him loose until they fix broken promises. My grandfather probably fighting Mexicans right now."

"Does anybody aboard this boat know what you are?"

Kraus grinned. "Only other Yaquis."

"Are there very many?" Joe asked.

"More than half."

So that was what the huge Indian who choked him had been getting at. Joe wondered if . . . *forget it!* The Mexican captain had already chickened out. Give him half an hour to save face and they'd all be turned loose with apologies.

Dr. Lilly climbed slowly from the upper bunk. He el-

bowed space on the floor and began exercising the stiffness
from his battered body. Enunciating carefully through puffy
lips, he asked, "Who supplies the arms for your war?"

"Gringos." Kraus said.

"So the Americans are your allies against the Mexican
oppressor?"

"No," Kraus said. "They just people sell guns and don'
ask where gold or cows come from."

Lilly's battered face flushed but he would not let it go.
"What's the word for Mexicans in your language?" he
asked.

"*Yorim,*" Kraus said. At that moment the cell door
opened. Gorson was back looking no worse than before and
now it was the security expert's turn.

"What happened to your yeoman—yeoperson?" Gorson
asked when he had found room to sit in the crowded cell.

Joe didn't know. He hoped she was being held somewhere
in more comfort and privacy. That would depend on how the
Mexicans interpreted a woman's role. *Soldaderas* had always been the army's only commissary, supply, and medical
corps. But in the navy . . ? "Did he get anything out of
you?" Joe asked.

Gorson grinned. "He wanted to know if Pistolilly here
was really loco."

Joe smiled. That meant the captain was searching for some
face-saving way to turn them loose. "Has anyone noticed if
this ship has radio?" he asked.

"Two antennas." Freedy struggled to adjust broken
glasses. "Chances are it's strictly Morse Code and key."

Joe sighed. There would be no way to undo the mischief
caused by this meddling in recent history . . . then Joe
recalled the captain's *Would you throw away tomorrow's
newspaper?* If that captain was greedy enough to keep the
news to himself . . . But what about the crew? To hell with
them. Rumors and gossip were part of the human condition.
If the captain held his tongue and filed no report maybe it
could all be smoothed over.

Joe wracked his brains to recall some bit of knowledge he

could offer the Mexican—some royal road to a fast peso. Abruptly he knew he had it. The twenties and thirties had not been a period of open fighting but there had been continual jockeying for position as politicians shot and poisoned one another. It would be worth a man's while to back a winner. He would tell the captain to attach himself to Cárdenas—now while the great man was still unknown. Joe was congratulating himself when, from somewhere down the companionway there was a sudden confused shouting.

The short sailor on guard at the door turned to look and his broad face abruptly disappeared in a splash of blood. Sound reechoed deafeningly in the passage. There were more shots and Joe knew different caliber weapons were being fired.

They cringed away from the cell door and possible ricochets, wishing for weapons, for freedom to move, for any number of things they did not have. Shouting reechoed amid shots and Joe could not tell if it was Spanish or Yaqui. Then during a lull in the shooting he understood. He looked around the cell and saw that only one man was missing. The missing man was out there shooting people up and yelling "¡Mueran los yorim! Kill the Mexicans!"

"You know," Gorson said. "That guy really is crazy."

There was a timberjuddering thump and Joe remembered the one-pounders on deck. He had no idea how Lilly had pulled it off but somehow the security man had managed to stir it all up again and get a few more people killed just when the captain had been searching his soul for some suitably decorous way to turn them loose and pretend it never happened.

Lilly could do a lot of damage, Joe supposed. But there was no way the weapons expert was going to take a whole ship without catching a round. "Sit quiet and well back from the door," Joe told his people. "Our friend out there is creating an excuse for them to kill the lot of us."

"Think he can do it?" Cook asked.

The heavy gun thumped again, sending a shudder through the brig, and then the shooting seemed to die down. They sat waiting to see who would come to the cell door.

Chapter 10

"Will it be the lady or the tiger?" Dr. Greybull asked.

Joe cursed himself for not having done what must be done with Lilly. No matter who came to the cell door, the bluff that Joe had almost pulled off was now ancient history—history that would never be the same if this shindy managed to get the United States into still another wrong war with the wrong country at the wrong time.

"Do you get the feeling that somebody's forgotten about us?" Gorson asked after a moment of tense silence.

"I do," Joe said. A battered tin cup fell off the bunk and rolled across the increasingly off-level deck of their cell. Joe felt sorriest for the new boys who'd never gotten a decent whack at life. "Been nice knowing all of you," he added.

"That all you got to say?" Gorson asked.

"I suppose I could add *shit,*" Joe said absently. His mind was on Margaret White.

"*Eli, eli,*" Rose growled. "Five thousand years and you still can't mind the store?"

They waited, each thinking his own long thoughts. Joe wondered if Margaret White would be loose somewhere and able to escape this sinking craft—and if she might not end up wishing she were dead like the rest of them.

"Apparently," Dr. Greybull said, "It will be neither lady nor tiger."

Then abruptly the huge grinning Indian was opening the cell door. He beckoned. They looked at the Indian and at each other.

"¿*Todos?*" Joe finally managed. "All of us?"

"Considering the list and the moisture I see advancing—" Dr. Greybull began. Their paralysis became a stampede through inchdeep water that sloshed over the companionway. The Indian was making no effort to guard them. Joe prayed there were no more crypto Lillys among his crew to screw up this new alliance.

On deck men lay dead and dying in unheroic postures. In the gap between the tied-together rum runner and the *Alice* a body was sinking. Another splashed over the side and then Joe saw it had not just fallen overboard, that the splash came from the terrier-shaking of jaws.

The blackhulled boat was down by the stern.

"Jesus!" Gorson observed.

Someone had depressed a one-pounder and fired it through the deck and out the transom stern just below the waterline.

Another body splashed and then the victors—Yaquis, Joe supposed—were lowering a mattress with ropes and boat hooks, struggling to plug the hole where the one-pounder had shattered transom planking.

Joe knew scuba gear had not been invented yet. But many coastal Indians were pearl divers. The men who perched over the stern prodding a mattress in place with boat hooks were not speaking Spanish. Neither were they going into the water alongside feeding sharks. Joe caught at the huge Indian who had choked him. "¿*Que pasó?*" he asked. "¿Is it that Yaquis now hold the boat, or does the Mexican captain still run things?"

The Indian grinned and pointed astern where sharks were feeding.

Joe knew he was responsible for this. If he had only steeled himself to do what must be done all these blameless men who were just doing their jobs would still be alive. And L.Cdr. Joseph Rate had not even the excuse that he had been following orders. The Indians were still throwing bodies over the side. "Why?" Joe asked. "Why did you have to kill them all?"

The huge Indian continued grinning as he yelled at a short dark sailor. Men began humping over a hand bilge pump on the afterdeck. Joe considered the angle at which the black-hulled boat lay and knew pumping would never do it. "Got any—" He couldn't remember the word for oakum. Maybe cotton waste would do. "¿estopas?" he demanded.

Kraus stuck his head up out of a hatch. "Down here," he yelled. "Blankets!"

They were up to their necks in water, Dr. Lilly in the midst of Indians, passing rags and cushions that a taller man struggled to ram in place with the tip of an oar. Joe pitched in and helped. Gorson's voice roared through the babble of Spanish and Yaqui, and a hose came down through a deck opening. More hoses came down and then every man who was not ramming rags into the hole was sucking water overboard with handy billys looted from the *Alice*.

Good thing they had been looted, Joe supposed. If this boat went down he would end up with all survivors aboard the *Alice*. He suspected too many men would be even less convenient than the superfluity of women on their last voyage. *My god, where was Margaret?* He had forgotten her.

All hands labored and finally it seemed to Joe that they were winning. As the water level in the stern of the rum runner descended he turned to his only Yaqui-speaking crewman. "Have you any idea what happened?"

"Lilly almos' ruin it," Kraus explained.

"Jumped the gun before they were quite ready," Joe supposed. "But why are the Indians so bitter against the Mexicans?"

Kraus turned to the huge Indian who had choked Joe and spoke in whistles and double vowels unlike any European tongue. The big man looked at Joe, and said, *"Mi canoa—"*

As he broke off Joe realized the Indian's Spanish was more limited than his own.

"He was fishing," Kraus interpreted. "This boat came along and draft him."

"And he lost his dugout?"

"His boy was ten. He could have paddled home."

Joe began to wish he hadn't asked.

"They shoot up boat so new sailor got no reason run away," Kraus continued.

Joe glanced astern where sharks circled and recalled what he had told the other captain. Someday Joe would pay his own debts. But for now he was still captain. "All hands!" he called as he came up on deck. "Let's get our gear back aboard before some other misunderstanding develops with our new friends. Anybody seen my yeoperson?"

Nobody had.

If they were to get away it had better be now while these freebooters were still full of good feeling and gratitude. How had Lilly managed it? Probably because the Indians were used to getting arms and help from Americans. Too bad men like Lilly couldn't be kept in mothballs. The security man was an everpresent danger—not just to the *Alice*, but to civilization. But could civilization survive without his kind? Could the *Alice* survive if Joe didn't get off the stick?

Lilly was still below, packing putty into cracks, nailing and screwing boards for a temporary patch. Joe went on deck and a short dark sailor was tugging at Margaret White. And thus it was Joe instead of Lilly who nearly ruptured the fragile alliance in the instant before he saw that the sailor was not interested in his yeoperson's person. The Indian wanted the armload of gear Margaret was packing into a sling to swing back aboard the *Alice*.

"*¡Espere un momento!*" Joe yelled. "We're going to pay you."

The Indian gave Joe the look of a man who's heard the great white father's promises before. Joe asked himself what he could give that might not be missed. He was still worrying when Gorson emerged from the lazarette where Margaret had hidden. He had 750 milliliters of whiskey in each hand.

Some damned lazarette where Gorson and Cookies' smuggling had gotten Joe in hot water years ago. There must be something freudian in the number of places he had not inspected. But it was Gorson's whiskey or Lilly's arms. The Indians would have no interest in anything else.

The short sailor was now helping Margaret load gear into the cargo sling. Joe went aft to the gaping door of the captain's cabin. He snatched a blanket from the bunk and began recovering things taken from his quarters. On the captain's desk was a hand tinted photograph of a darkhaired woman with two children. Joe thanked the fates that he had never married or engendered hostages to fortune. He reminded himself that the huge Indian had neither pictures nor son.

With the skill of an experienced bartender Gorson was rationing out enough whiskey to keep everyone happy aboard the blackhulled boat, while quietly promising an agonizing death to any of the *Alice's* people who partook.

Cook and Freedy inventoried and reported that everything of lasting importance was once more aboard the ketch, including Dr. Greybull's suitcaseful of malfunctioning electronics.

"Can you make it work this time?" Joe asked.

The graybearded scientist shrugged. "Your people invented it. Do you understand it?"

Joe stared. "Don't you?"

"No more than Einstein understood general relativity."

"Then why did you let those Washington—people—drag you into this crazy business?"

"To get along, you go along. I needed funding for a project that interested me."

"Looks like we got 'bout all we're gonna git, Mr. Rate," Cook reported.

Mutineers aboard the blackhulled boat had settled into a bonhomie punctuated with occasional warwhoops, save for two who still labored belowdecks with Dr. Lilly, packing putty into the shot-through transom. The transom already bore the marks of repairs from the time Lilly had put a heatseeking rocket up an exhaust pipe.

Lilly seemed devoted to his job down there. Not eager to come on deck and face the consequences of his rashness, Joe supposed. Nor could the security expert be totally insensitive to the rents he had torn in the fabric of time. If ever they came home how would this incident have affected the balance of power in the world? Very little Joe realized, if the Mexican captain had been lax enough or greedy enough not to radio his headquarters. But what if someone believed the Indians' wild boasts once they hit the mainland? What if this was the pivotal incident that triggered another, perhaps this time successful Indian revolt and sent white civilization packing back to Europe?

Lilly was doing a conscientious job. Must be several pounds of putty plastered over the shattered transom, worked into neat fillets to prevent water from leaking between loosened planking and the exhaust pipe. Some marine archaeologist might someday wonder just how all this fast-setting space-age muck got into a boat destined to sink or rot before it was invented.

"Lilly," Joe called. "Don't you think you've done enough?"

There was a tight smile in the ascetic planes and angles of the security expert's face as he came up out of the hold. "Do you?" he asked.

Joe sensed that Lilly knew Joe considered him expendable.

"Are we forgetting anything?" Joe asked Gorson.

"What about the bottles we came for?" Lilly asked with that same tight smile. "Looks like we're giving more glass than we're getting."

Joe shrugged. "Did anyone see the slightest sign of a bell jar or a five gallon jug or anything we could use?"

Nobody had.

"Haul in those fenders," Joe said. "Our allies may change their minds."

Abe Rose laughed. "The good old 400 horsepower Liberty was a V-12 engine," he said.

"Don't you mean *is*?" Joe asked.

"Not after you've dinged the spark plug threads on one bank."

Joe stared.

"They'll run," Rose explained. "Once those Indians sober up they can get back to land. But, hitting on every other cylinder, those engines won't be fast enough to play pirate."

The blackhulled boat now floated at her proper angle. If the Indians tended to business there was no reason why they should sink. "They'll make it ok," Joe said. Abruptly he wondered what had happened to Kraus. Then he saw the latino helping Hennis aboard the *Alice*." The black seemed to be hurting more now.

"Those valiant freedom fighters will accomplish their rendezvous with destiny." Lilly was still smiling.

Joe could not see what was so amusing about undisciplined people with weapons and a boat they just might know how to repair. He recalled Kraus's "My grandfather is probably at war with Mexicans right now."

Greybull saw Joe's worry. "Unfinished business," he muttered.

"And not all in its due time." Joe was still worrying when the sundown calm ended and a gentle breeze filled the *Alice's* sails.

Looking tired and drawn, Margaret White appeared. "Are you all right?" she asked.

Joe gave a guilty start. It was the question he should have been asking her. "Yeah. How about you? Did they—"

"Kept me locked in a cabin a ways forward of yours," she said. "They all seemed a little bit afraid of me. Or maybe of you," she added.

Joe felt a sudden surge of unearned pride.

Lilly was still glinting with secret amusement. Joe knew

that sooner or later he would be enlightened. He was sure he was not going to find it nearly as amusing as the good doctor. What *was* he to do with Lilly? Owed him a commendation for sparking the mutiny. But if the security man had not johnwayned onto the deck of a patrol boat that had been about to offer them a tow . . .

Gorson stared forebodingly at the blackhulled boat now merging into gathering darkness. "I hope you're right about how slow those engines will move her," he said. Rose shrugged and began checking battery-condition indicators in the *Alice's* cockpit. He was reaching to turn on the motor when the nightfall change of wind direction began heeling the ketch over.

One of the new boys hopped to grasp the makeshift tiller. The *Alice* lay over on her lines and began sailing. "Away?" Syverson asked.

Joe studied the blackhulled rum runner a half mile alee and saw what Gorson had been seeing. Black smoke from an out-of-tune engine billowed astern. Blue-yellow flashes and the popping of unburned fuel came across the gentle swell toward them and then there was a larger flash. Three seconds later the *Alice's* standing rigging thrummed in a wave of concussion.

A backstay twanged and the mainmast groaned in its socket. Joe leaped for the jury-rigged tiller but the new boy was already turning up into the wind before more damage could be done. There are seldom any echoes at sea but as Joe aimed binoculars at the blazing patch of gasoline where the blackhulled boat had been it seemed to him that the explosion was rumbling on much too long.

"Son of a bitch!" Gorson muttered.

Joe lowered the binoculars and suddenly saw the reason behind Lilly's smile. There would be fewer loose ends this way—less damage to the time stream from an unreported boat. But now Joe knew why Lilly had worked so willingly—and what kind of plastic Dr. Lilly had been using to plug that leaky transom.

How long it would take Kraus to figure it out?

Chapter 11

The *Alice's* people goggled as the sea lit up. Joe knew immediately that any loose ends from that colossal eruption of flame would be tied up by sharks or drowning before the ketch could pay off and reach back. He was sickly aware that those were real people out there, with real problems that would never be solved now. Rescue was hopeless but he had to go through the motions. "Rose! Have you done anything about that backstay yet?"

"It'll hold for now," the engineman said.

"Hard over!" Joe yelled. "All hands topside to look for survivors."

Dr. Greybull's eyes flicked from Lilly to Joe. The scientist's face was noncommittal as gasoline mushroomed, then spread and subsided. With the wind abaft on a broad reach the *Alice* made it back just as the gasoline puddle emitted its final flickering *whump*. The explosion had been even more thorough than Joe had imagined. Save for splinters and small bits of scorched cork from life jackets, nothing floated.

Gorson took in sail and they motored for several passes

across the oil slick that marked the limits of the fire. Finally, honor was satisfied. Joe ordered the *Alice* back on her original course. He had no real idea how far offshore they were, or how many ships the Mexican *Guardacostas* possessed but common sense dictated that they get the hell out of here.

Kraus was still stunned.

"Take the helm," Joe told him. "I'll send you a relief as soon as we get things sorted out and stored."

The boy nodded dazedly but did not speak as he stepped up to the cobbled-up tiller. Kraus gave a final expressionless stare at the burned-out gasoline slick, then glanced from the dimlit portable compass to the sky. When he had picked his star and began ignoring the swinging compass card the *Alice* settled down on her lines. The crew pitched in to get the clutter belowdecks before it could go skittering over the side.

Joe was stowing calculator and books in his cabin when there was an abrupt rattlesnap of canvas as the ketch shifted tacks without warning, pitching him headfirst into his bunk. He lay for a frozen instant waiting for the snap of another stay, the crack of the mainmast.

Gorson beat him to the cabin slide by a nose. By the time they were in the cockpit the *Alice* was back on the starboard tack and starting to heel again. The steersman was alone, nobody having thought to post a watch. The dim reflection of the compass light hit Kraus from below, giving his face the eery shadows of a budget horror movie.

"What happened?" Joe demanded. "What'd you almost hit?"

The boy did not answer. Joe repeated the question and got no reaction. Joe sighed. Probably Kraus was wondering if any of those Indians had been in his immediate family line. Shouldn't have put him on the wheel. But would it have been more kind to leave the kid with nothing to do?

The breeze was still freshening. As the *Alice* heeled with her port rail awash Gorson fiddled with the roller-reefing controls for a moment, then went below. Joe glanced at the patent taffrail log and discovered their speed was zero. He cursed the mutual antipathy between the works of man and the salts of the sea. But when he twisted it the log shaft turned freely. The line out to the tiny propeller a hundred feet astern was taut but the line was not turning, which meant the spinner had picked up another gob of seaweed.

Joe wished the inventor of the patent log into the low rent section of hell as he began hauling in the line. He knew it was weed because whenever a swordfish discovered the spinner was inedible it usually destroyed the whole machine.

Salt water and thin line dug into his office-soft hands as he hauled in and heard the swash of something just under the rail. As he bent over to grab it a claw emerged from the darkness and grabbed Joe.

Abruptly Joe discovered that terror can overcome apathy. Taken in the abstract, he was sick of life and wouldn't mind—but not this way! Not just at this moment! The helmsman was only a couple of yards away. Joe struggled to yell and managed only to emit an asthmatic whistle. He gripped the rail and fought to free himself. Another hand grabbed him and then a man was climbing up over Joe and onto the deck. "Can't you make up your mind?" Lilly asked.

Joe stared, struggling to recover from the panic that had muted him. What sterile intellectualism had ever convinced him that he was ready to die? Then he understood that Lilly was not talking philosophy. Involuntarily, Joe glanced at the helmsman. Kraus held his head high, steering by a star.

"Oh." Lilly's voice was quiet.

"Did somebody push you overboard?" It was a stupid question but Joe had to ask.

Dripping, Dr. Lilly stepped down into the footdeep cockpit and faced Kraus. The security man's face was in darkness. The latino boy's was still lit from beneath by the makeshift compass light. Kraus gave Lilly an incurious glance, then looked back up to his star and twitched the tiller. Lilly stood motionless for an eternity that could not have exceeded five seconds, then turned and disappeared below.

Joe was losing control of his ship and his crew. He had to do something. But what? He tried to remember the personnel jackets he had looked over. Kraus was still a month short of nineteen. Had there been anyone else on deck?

"I was resting and gathering strength," Lilly said when Joe went below.

Joe stared at the weapons man, struggling to make some sense of what he was saying. "There seems to be a missing line in this text," Joe finally said.

"It is possible that I do not owe you my life," Lilly explained, "but that point will be ever moot." He had changed into dry clothing and sat nursing a heavy handleless mug of coffee that smelled of Wild Turkey.

"Odd how things work out sometimes," Joe said.

"Going to do anything about it?"

"I'm afraid Macbeth would never play in Indian country."

Lilly raised his eyebrows. "I believe *your* printer's skipping lines."

"Banquo's ghost didn't get you much of a reaction now, did it?"

"I suppose I'll have to do it myself." Lilly shrugged. "We have our ways."

"Not on my ship you don't !"

Lilly grinned. "You shouldn't have rescued me."

"Nobody's perfect." Joe retreated to his cabin before he could finish hanging himself.

Margaret White sat on the bunk, arms wrapped around her knees, wearing Joe's dungarees and one of his T-shirts. His clothing looked nicer on her than on him. "Are you all right?" she asked.

"What are you doing here?"

"You told me to stay until—"

"I'm sorry. I remember now." Although the navy had gone coed the fo'c's'l of the *Alice* had been designed before the era of equality. Where was he going to put her?

"I can sleep in that hole where you found me."

"The lazarette?"

"Is that what you call it? It could be nice and comfortable with a mattress and some way to bolt the hatch from inside."

Joe had a sudden vision of how cozy it could be in that snug compartment with a wellfilled pair of dungarees. He reminded himself that his yeoperson's life had already been complicated by unwanted attentions and that, like it or not, he was her superior officer. So what was he to do?

A gallant captain would give his own quarters to a maiden in distress—and play musical chairs with his officers. But Joe's was the only cabin aboard the ketch. He could not work the ship without his chart table and other appurtenances of the navigator. Lilly and Greybull were already crowding crew's quarters.

"I'm sorry," she said.

"Don't apologize. I don't think you'll have any trouble but be careful."

"It's Dr. Lilly who worries me."

Joe felt a sudden and totally irrational surge of fury. "Is he bothering you?"

Margaret shook her head. "Not that way."

Joe remembered that she had stowed away to escape a charge of murder.

"I don't think he even likes women," she added.

"Doesn't think much of men either," Joe agreed.

There was a knock and the door opened without waiting. Dr. Greybull had shaved around the edges of his beard and seemed less used-up. "Excuse me," he said as he saw Margaret.

"I was just leaving." She scooted past him.

"Decidedly awkward," Greybull said when she was gone.

Joe decided the old man was trying to be friendly. At least he wasn't smirking. "What can I do for you?"

"There's a question of our original mission," Greybull began.

"Surely you jest. Or didn't Lilly manage to deep-six all your spare glassware?"

"I'm afraid he did," the scientist said.

"Then we can't even get home, much less to the 4th century."

"It's all just magic, you know."

Joe had sometimes suspected as much. But if one defined magic as imperfectly understood science . . . "Are you familiar with medieval accounts of Brother Soandso who experimented with forbidden things until the Devil carried him off, body and soul, in a tremendous clap of thunder?"

Greybull nodded. "I can sympathize with the poor abbot trying to raise funds for still another gunpowder experiment." The old man sat on the edge of the bunk and studied Joe. "Do you know anything of physics?"

"I was once an historian."

"That's non sequitur."

"Is it? History never repeats itself but there are recurrent patterns. Is the Theory of Relativity less absurd than some ancient theological squabble over an iota that we're supposed to rearrange?"

"Relativity works." Greybull said.

"Does it now? The sacred text reveals that nothing can surpass the speed of light. But what of those heretics who keep pointing out that gravity must be faster than light if galaxies are not to fly apart just as the somewhat larger universe seems to be doing? And what of Michelson and Morley? All through school I was told they found no ether-drift and therefore there's no ether."

Greybull studied Joe in quizzical silence.

"Their experiment has been verified, refined and published a dozen times in the last century," Joe said, "and still the results are ignored. Is it because eight kilometers a second instead of the predicted sixty just refuses to squeeze into either theory? Please, doctor, dance me no angels on that pinhead."

"The data," Greybull said wryly, "come closer to proving Earth is the center of a ptolemaic universe and that everything revolves around us. In any event, what has this to do with time travel?"

"I'm no expert." Joe said, "but even a layman sees that orthodox science is increasingly hemmed in by indicators of faster-than-light phenomena: gravity waves—you name it. If something can move faster than light, then relativity and spacetime have as much relevance as prayer.''

''You argue my case most eloquently.'' Greybull's grin was almost as disconcerting as Lilly's.

''Magic?'' Joe echoed.

''Or imperfectly understood science. All I say is that your original machine worked better than all our improvements. I can't help believing it's more to do with the operator than—''

''*Credo quia absurdum,*'' Joe muttered. Then abruptly he thought of something else. ''Have you any idea what language they'll speak at the Council of Nicaea?''

''Weren't you just speaking it?''

''Afraid not,'' Joe said. ''There was a time when I knew Latin fairly well. Homeric Greek too. But koine . . . I suppose I could bungle through enough to buy a bottle of retsina.''

''What's koine?''

Joe stared. ''The experts in Washington sent you and you can't speak New Testament Greek either?''

Dr. Greybull's mouth opened but he had nothing to say. To Joe it seemed pointless to recall how ''carefully it had all been worked out.'' They sat in silence for a moment while Joe's sailor half noted that the *Alice* had heeled slightly beyond her best sailing angle and was obviously overcanvassed in a freshening breeze. He was squeezing past Greybull to see why nobody was minding the store when there came an odd little jolt and canvas flapped until the ketch came about on a new heading. As the *Alice* settled down again he noted that the wind was not so strong.

''Gorson!'' Joe bawled.

Gorson and Cook were busy with a handy billy pump and a plastic bucket on the galley table. Makeshift coax created with wire-in-hose-in-pipe ran from the apparatus on the table to the fathometer where Freedy held broken glasses to his nose while twiddling range switches.

Gorson looked up sweaty and tired. ''Sorry, Joe,'' he said. ''I guess it isn't gonna work.''

Joe charged through the galley and up the cabin slide. It took him a moment to adjust to the darkness and then he saw that Kraus was still on the wheel.

Kraus seemed confused as he studied compass and stars to orient himself.

"What happened?" Joe asked.

"I don' know," Kraus said.

Joe studied the sky. Polaris still lay some 25° above the horizon but it was the wrong time of night or the wrong time of year. An hour ago Orion had been overhead.

"Didn't you feel it?" Joe demanded when Gorson and Cook had followed him on deck.

"Thought I felt a little twinge," Cook conceded. "But we were hopin' for more. You got any idea when we are?"

"Not even where," Joe sighed, "but we're on the same latitude."

While Gorson shortened sail to bare steerageway and set a new watch Joe went below. One of these days, he thought forebodingly, we'll use up our probabilities. Even if Earth is mostly ocean, we're going to end up on dry land. He looked at Freedy.

The radioman shook his head. "Close to a hundred fathoms," he said, "But not a flicker on the radio."

"That puts us at least a century back." Lilly seemed recovered from his dunking.

"Marconi wasn't bouncing them across the Atlantic until 1901," Dr. Greybull said, "and there wasn't much real long distance traffic until World War I. We could still be in the twenties."

"We *may* still be in the past," Joe said glumly. "But what kind of future are we building?"

"Any future would have electromagnetic communications," Lilly protested.

"And fusion bombs," Joe added. "Perhaps the lungfish will make a better job of it if he dwelleth not in the shadow of gamma."

"What on earth are you talking about?"

"Extinction." Joe remembered that he had promised the Mexican captain immortality as the destroyer of his country.

Chapter 12

Lilly and Greybull stared at Joe. Only the weapons expert grinned. "Have you reason to believe we might be in the future?" Dr. Greybull finally asked.

"No reason. Just experience."

Gorson glanced up from the makeshift apparatus. "Way this thing usually works, doc," he began, "Is, it takes some power—lightning—to get us into the past and that always blows up the coil. Seems like it doesn't take near as much power to jerk us back into our own time."

"Comin' back never blew up the still," Cook added.

"A still?" Lilly said. "Aboard a navy ship?"

The whole time travel industry had spun off Gorson and Cook's experiments with vacuum distillation of raisin jack. "Yes, a still," Joe said pointedly. "And the product is less appetizing than Wild Turkey."

"Lemme see what you got left in that suitcase," Gorson urged.

"That's private property!" Lilly bristled.

"Screw you!" Gorson snapped. "I want Dr. Greybull's time machine."

"Why not?" the older man said. "You're having more luck than I am."

Joe went back on deck to hunt for a planet with a periodicity long enough to extrapolate a time fix. It took Pluto 248 years to make it once around the sun. It also took something stronger than a sextant to find Pluto. There was something out of place up there. Could be Saturn or maybe Jupiter. Why hadn't he done his homework and given Washington a list of the things he needed—like a good telescope and some occultation tables for the Galilean satellites?

Kraus was on the helm again, holding the ketch on the wind and paying scant attention to compass or stars. Which made sense, Joe supposed, as long as nobody knew where they were going.

"See anything?" he asked.

"*Nada.*"

There was a change in Kraus. Joe remembered how he had dissembled before Lilly. Yet Kraus was now just a boy again. It required no talent to see that he was lying.

"Nothing at all?" Joe pressed.

Kraus shrugged and indicated the sea and the stars. Since Joe had been below the east had brightened noticeably. He glanced automatically at his watch and gritted his teeth. If he knew the time and date he could calculate longitude. If he knew his longitude he could work out Greenwich mean time but without one or the other even the most brilliant mathematician was sucking wind.

"Give me a yell when it looks like the sun's about to come up," he said. He was preparing to go below again when abruptly Joe knew why Kraus was lying. He took a final turn around deck and almost stumbled over the lookout who lay prone in the bows.

Jim Syverson had an open freckled face and red hair. For an instant Joe suspected his lookout had been sleeping but the boy's voice was alert. "You see it, sir?"

The eastern horizon was getting lighter by the minute. Joe squinted where Syverson was pointing and made out the silhouette of a small craft under sail. Syverson handed him the binoculars. Joe got them into focus, wondering once again who kept screwing them so far out of whack, and finally achieved a faint double image of a dugout with a single occupant. Joe looked away and breathed deeply for a moment. A human being!

He had not destroyed the world—yet.

The mast was short and the boom high and long, creating a V shaped sail with the wide part at the top as Joe had occasionally seen on double hulled *va'a* in the South Pacific. That was impossible. Then he remembered that the "South Pacific" extended well into the northern hemisphere and that he was not all that far off the latitude of the Hawaiian Islands. But the Hawaiians had abandoned this sailing rig two centuries ago. He glanced back at Kraus and knew the helmsman had seen the man in the dugout. Joe suspected he knew why the half-Indian had held his tongue.

"Do you recognize the rig?" he asked.

Kraus shook his head. "Some kind fishing boat," he guessed.

"Afraid of him?"

Kraus concentrated on his steering.

"Or afraid of what we might do to him?"

Kraus gave Joe a sudden sharp glance and abruptly Joe knew Lilly's guess had been right. "Follow him," Joe said.

"He kill you."

"Who?"

"The man in the boat."

"You know him?"

Kraus did not reply.

"I'm not recruiting like those other poor bastards," Joe said. "I just want to ask where and when we are."

Kraus gave Joe a doubtful look but he swung the tiller until the ketch fell off on a beam reach. Joe experimented with the electric controls and trimmed sheets until she settled down. By the time they neared the man in the dugout the sun was half an hour high and the ground swell nauseating enough to have alerted everyone that they were in shallow water.

Freedy stuck his head up out of the cabin slide. "Ten fathoms," he called, "and shoaling out."

The smudge to the east had resolved into a low patchwork of greens and browns. The fisherman had been sailing for shore when first they sighted him. In the course of the chase he had fussed with his primitive sail and done his best to get more speed from the dugout but he had obviously soon realized he would never reach shore before the *Alice* could intercept him.

Through the binoculars Joe saw a brownskinned man in loincloth and straw hat with sparse chinwhiskers and mustache. His black hair hung in short braids with hanks of red and white cotton yarn intertwined. He had an ornately carved steering paddle.

As the *Alice* caught up and its wind shadow collapsed the dugout's inverted sail the man drew his paddle inboard and waited. "Any chance of you speaking English?" Joe yelled.

Of course not.

Joe looked at his small feet and knew this man was no Polynesian. He tried again in Spanish. There seemed a glint of intelligence in middle aged eyes but the man in the dugout did not reply. Abruptly Joe realized it hadn't worked after all. In spite of Gorson and Cook's horsing around with fathometer and coils and plastic buckets and bilge pump vacuums they were still off the west coast of Mexico. He must have imagined that flicker.

"See if you can get through," he told Kraus.

"*Em chiokwe, achai,*" Kraus shouted.

"*Em chianabu,*" the man in the dugout replied.

"More Yaquis?" Lilly asked.

"Go below, stay below, and don't show your face until I send for you," Joe said.

Lilly grinned but did not reply as he disappeared down the cabin slide.

Kraus was having heavy going with the man in the dugout. Gorson manned the makeshift tiller, holding the hove-to Alice windward of the smaller craft.

"Doesn't he understand Spanish?" Joe demanded. "I thought all Yaquis could speak Spanish."

Kraus gave Joe an unfathomable look. "He says his people raid for horses but they don't let *yorim* in the valley."

"Oho!" It was Abe Rose talking around an eternal cigar.

"You know something?" Joe asked.

"There are certain parallels with a culture with which I have a nodding acquaintance," the engineman said.

"I don't suppose he'd know any of the place names on a modern map," Joe hazarded.

"Try Mazatlan," Rose suggested.

Without hesitation the Indian pointed a little east of south.

Kraus seemed surprised. "You talk Yaqui?" he asked the engineman.

Rose shrugged. "According to the travel folders Mazatlan originally meant deer-place. Of course, he may just be steering us onto good hunting."

"I think I know where we are," Joe said. "I'm more interested in when."

"Ask if he's Christian."

Kraus received an emphatic and angry "*Kaita!*" as the Indian shook his head.

"That ties it to sometime after the Spaniards first discovered these Injuns took God Almighty's grant deed seriously," Rose said. "The Rio Yaqui delta was *their* promised land."

"When were they conquered?" Joe asked.

"Never!" Kraus was indignant.

"Then they're still not Christian?"

"Oh yes." Kraus was suddenly out of his depth.

"Each time the Spaniards tried they got their asses whupped," Rose explained. "But the Yaquis were catching hell too so they made a deal: priests could come but no soldiers. The Jesuits learned the quickest way to run up the score was to teach ironworking and gunsmithing in exchange for new Christian souls." Rose grinned. "If we'd had iron before the Philistines you can bet Samson would never have ended up eyeless in Gaza."

"When'd the Jesuits get in?" Joe asked.

"1617, I think."

"And Cortez landed in 1519," Joe mused. More impor-
tantly, he saw that a new factor had been added to time travel
This was the second—perhaps third time they had gone into
the past without tapping a lightning bolt.

The Indian was holding up a fish. "Wants trade," Kraus
said. Joe noted that the boy's English tended to break down
when he thought in another language. And communication
could not be all that easy between an uncorrupted Indian and
a 3-centuries-later descendant who spoke a language full of
Spanish words for all the things that had not existed before
the gun god.

"What's he want?" Joe asked.

"Water so he can stay out and catch more fish."

"Surely he wants more than that."

"He's too polite," Kraus explained.

Joe thought a moment. "Syverson, go below and tell Dr.
Lilly to issue you one knife from his no doubt abundant
stores. Something with a floating handle might be appropriate."

The Indian had fish and a hawkbilled sea turtle in his
dugout. When he saw the knife his eyes lit up in highly
unstoical delight and he forced his entire catch onto the *Alice*.

"Guess we can freeze some," Cook muttered. Joe suspected anything from this ocean would be tastier than the
iodized cardboard that results from the thawings and refreez-
ings of 20th century technology.

Kraus turned to Joe with a look of blank amazement. "He
wants us follow him."

It was Joe's turn to stare. A gift of a knife was one thing.
To invite powerful strangers with unknown motivations into
one's village was something else. "Did he say why?"

"I don' understand too good," Kraus said. "Something
about wise woman. I think his mother."

Joe looked at Abe Rose.

The engineman chewed his cigar and shrugged. "Some

matriarchal Indians down in Tehuantepec,'' he said, ''but Yaquis are strictly male chauvinist pigs.''

''We have our mission,'' Dr. Greybull said.

''I don't need anyone to remind me,'' Joe snapped.

There was an abrupt shimmer and then the sun was shining steadily again on a sea just like that of a moment before only the sun was higher and it was midmorning or midafternoon. Joe spun and dived down the slide.

Dr. Lilly looked up and grinned. He had been fiddling with the time machine that Gorson and Cook had cobbled up out of a handy billy and a plastic bucket. ''Looks like we're going to make it after all,'' the weapons man said.

Joe wondered if he would have to put Lilly in irons for the remainder of the cruise. ''Come on deck,'' he snapped.

The dugout had been nosed bow up to the *Alice* and it took Joe an instant to see that the sternmost third of the Indian's boat was neatly sliced off and missing. Kraus was staring accusingly at Joe.

''I'm sorry,'' Joe said. ''I didn't mean to kidnap the poor bastard. But I don't know how I'm going to explain what happened to him.''

The Indian, who should have been awestruck at such magic, was grinning as he climbed aboard the *Alice*. ''*Tu'i*,'' he said. ''*Tu'i, tu'i!*''

Joe turned to Kraus, wondering if the boy realized they had time jumped again. Had to. Dugouts didn't just slice themselves in two.

''He says, *good, good*.'' Kraus seemed as puzzled as Joe.

Chapter 13

The Indian lugged his yard-long hawkbill turtle to the bows of the *Alice* and whacked it smartly on the head with a belaying pin. Within minutes he had sliced the bottom shell loose and was tossing viscera to seagulls which had appeared from nowhere. Unconcerned with the loss of his dugout, the Indian devoted himself to cutting the turtle into bitesized chunks which he brought aft, using the concave carapace as a tray.

"Ain't never cooked turtle," Cook protested. "Anybody know how?"

"Make soup," Kraus said.

Cook surveyed the bloody gobbets doubtfully. "Hope somebody likes it," he said as he went below.

"Have you any idea when we are?" Dr. Greybull asked. "Could it be just a month or so like that second jump?"

"Hardly." Joe explained how they had bracketed their guest into the 98 year interval between the Spanish conquest and the arrival of the Jesuits. "Looks like the sun's still on the way up," he added with a touch of irrelevance.

Margaret White was asleep on his bunk when he went below. She looked tired. In his oversized dungarees she also seemed more vulnerable and defenseless than Joe had ever imagined his yeoperson could be. He stood looking at her for a moment, hardpressed to recall that she had disabled one attacker and killed another. What would she do to Joe if she awoke suddenly and found him looking down on her? Sooner or later he would have to dig up a mattress so she could bunk in the lazarette. But right now he needed the sextant.

They were not on the same latitude—or not in the same month. Without knowing the season he could not get a latitude until night when he could shoot Polaris—providing he was still in the northern hemisphere. He put the sextant away. This time Margaret was awake. "Are you all right?" she asked.

"Why do you keep asking that?"

"I don't know. You seem tired, I guess. Where are we?"

"Somewhere on one of Earth's oceans." Saying it, Joe knew he wasn't even sure of that. He went back on deck and scooped a handful of water from the lee rail. The water was salt. It was too salty.

Gorson saw him and tasted the water too. "What's your choice?" the bos'n asked. "Red Sea, Persian Gulf, or the Med?"

Joe shrugged and stared ahead. The sun promised to burn off the haze in another hour but for now he could not see more than a mile. The wave fetch was short, which meant the wind came off land somewhere closeby. The total lack of ground swell suggested they were in deep water.

"Search me," Rose was saying around his eternal cigar. Joe turned and found his engineman talking to Kraus. "A thousand miles south of Yaqui country they didn't exactly have queens but even now—I mean in our own time—women run things in Tehuantepec. Matriarchy's fairly common with Indians but I never heard of it among your people."

"Me neither," Kraus agreed.

"So don't ask me about your Old Wise Woman. If she's

his mother, why not ask him?'' Rose pointed at the newly acquired Indian who was exploring the *Alice* just as if he hadn't just lost his own dugout and ended up among strangers.

Baakot, which Kraus thought meant 'snake', was gradually noticing that the water around the *Alice* did not behave like the brackish Colorado-River-diluted Sea of Cortez. *''Hákuni?''* he asked.

Kraus turned to Joe. ''Wants to know where we are.''

''Tell him the truth,'' Joe said.

''You mean about time travel and everything?''

''Including that we don't know where or when we are.''

Kraus struggled to explain time in a language that had borrowed the Spanish word after priests and bells came to dole out snippets of this alien concept. He turned despairingly to Joe and asked, ''Why isn't he younger or older?''

''Because the magic doesn't work that way,'' Joe said. ''Tell him we'll try to get him home.''

''He don' want to go home.''

This struck Joe as odd until he remembered that he had not been all that keen on going home either—the first time. But this man was older and should have some connections. An outcast? Greed and need to attach himself to the munificent giver-of-knives? Or just a curious and carefree soul?

Margaret appeared in the cabin slide and the Indian's reaction gave no hint of matriarchy. He turned to Joe with a questioning sound.

Kraus was embarrassed. ''He wants to know if she belong you,'' the boy finally said.

''Commander,'' Margaret began.

Abruptly Joe knew there was something else wrong. He went to give her a hand up the ladder into the cockpit. ''Dr. Lilly's in your cabin,'' she murmured.

''I'll kill that son of a—!''

''No!'' she hastened. ''He asked me to tell you he needs to confer privately at your earliest convenience. I'm quoting,'' she added after a wry pause.

Joe studied the *Alice's* deck and knew there might never be a better time. "What can I do for you?" he asked when he found Lilly sitting in the single chair in his cabin.

"I think we're there," Lilly said.

"Where?"

"Where we started for. 3rd century A.D."

"What makes you think that?"

"Call it a hunch," the security man said.

There was a knock and Dr. Greybull crowded into the tiny cabin. "So you did it." He was addressing Lilly.

"We can't be sure till after dark," Lilly said.

Joe studied the security man. "Do you know how to take a star sight?"

Lilly nodded.

"Do you know some way of establishing longitude when we don't know the century or time of year?"

"Afraid that's beyond me," Lilly said. "Apart from the obvious method of backtracking from a landfall."

"What makes you so sure we're in the right time?"

"Because I operated the machine."

"Told you it was magic," Greybull murmured.

When Joe stared the older man continued, "In the lab we got unpredictable results. When eventually it did put someone into the middle of last week he went rather predictably insane running into himself every time he opened a door or turned a corner." Greybull paused and stroked his neat gray beard. "Finally it occurred to me that the people were all technicians and timesavers. Nobody believed or cared if the contraption would ever work."

"Then why'd it work for us?" Joe asked.

Dr. Greybull sighed. "I try to avoid that subject. It makes me sound like a bitter old man."

"Failure of will," Dr. Lilly said.

Joe recalled that the Director, whom Lilly resembled enough to raise suspicions of bastardy, was looked upon in some circles as an expert on will.

"But all we wanted was to get home," Joe protested.

"Really?" Greybull was smiling. "I'd think an historian would vow his virility for such an experience."

He was right. Joe would never have come back if he hadn't felt responsible to the *Alice* and her people. "But I never ran the machine," he protested. "Gorson and Cook used to handle it."

"Young men. Fresh from a relatively good war and not really ready to settle down," Greybull mused. "I suspect your machine is like the genie of Arab legend. It grants not the wish you clamor for, but instead gives some darker Freudian version of what's really festering several layers beneath the id."

"It's disquieting to accept magic," Joe said.

"Your Indian up on deck lives complacent in a world of unexplained phenomena," Lilly said. "Did you note how easily he took it all in?"

Lilly was acting almost human. Joe wondered if the near-closed eye and impression of a boat hook on the side of his head had anything to do with why the weapons man no longer exuded his aura of silent menace that raised everyone's hackles. Joe forced himself to consider Lilly's suggestion. Primitives did not expect the universe to be explainable or improvable. Like Lilly, they took it as it came. "You think we're in the proper era because you wanted badly to get there and because you operated the machine?" Joe asked.

"It got *you* where you wanted to go. Even if you didn't operate the machine you were the only one aboard with a reasonable knowledge of history." Lilly paused. "You were a budding young assistant professor. The rest of the crew knew nothing except that the big adventure in their lives had just ended and they didn't really want to go back home yet. Your detailed knowledge prevailed."

"But magic, for Christ's sake!" Joe protested.

There were voices out in the galley. Joe opened the door and saw Freedy at the radar. The electronics man pushed his glasses back up his nose and looked at Joe. He shrugged and shook his head. Joe closed the door again.

Lilly's hard grin flashed. "Are your objections of a religious nature?"

"What?"

"Magic," Lilly said. " 'Thou shalt not suffer a witch to live.' forbids the practice of magic but seems not to deny its existence. I can't recall the Bible's exact words on the topic of free will."

Dr. Greybull stroked his beard and kept his peace.

"Free will," Joe said, "Is God's ingenious little way to void a warranty. Even if it's not the best proposition in town, his Opponent guarantees that a deal's a deal."

Lilly's battered face almost smiled. "Even a Jesuit finds it difficult in this century to take satanism seriously." He studied Joe for a moment. "Surely you're not a predestinarian—infant damnation and all that?"

"My view of the cosmos is less optimistic than all that grim Caledonian crap," Joe said.

"A solipsist?"

"My world ends the day I die—just as yours will for you."

"But surely you believe in something?"

Lilly was leading him in a direction Joe did not want to go. "Great evil," he finally said, "is the inevitable result of great belief. I try to keep my convictions small." He surveyed the man he would sooner or later have to kill and tried to change the subject. "Why did you volunteer for this mission?"

"I didn't. You're the man kept wanting to go."

"Then why are you here?"

"For God and Country," Lilly said, "and possibly because I had a Jesuit education."

Joe's mouth opened.

"You may disagree with them," Lilly said, "but I never heard any complaints about Jesuit scholarship."

"Then you know at least something about the era we're tinkering with."

"Would you like it in Latin?" Lilly asked, "or would you prefer the language in which St. Paul wrote the New Testament?"

There was a knock and Gorson opened the door. "Fog's burning off," he said. "There's land east of us. Shipping lanes are kind of busy too."

Joe beat the others up the cabin slide. Gorson pointed to a square sail emerging from the fog a mile astern. Ahead loomed another sail, barely filling in the light air as it crossed the *Alice's* bow. Joe snatched the binoculars and studied it. The one ahead was not a warship.

The hull was not as long as the *Alice* but would have three times its carrying capacity, thanks to tubby lines. The rig was a single square sail on a stubby mast and would not sail into the wind for sour apples. Where the bowsprit belonged was a carved goose head and neck. The stern rose in a stylized representation of the same bird's stubby tail.

"Any idea when or where?" Dr. Greybull asked.

"A real expert could pin it down," Joe said. "Best I could say is 300 BC to ditto AD."

"Is it Greek?"

"It looks like one of those freighters the Romans used to haul Egyptian grain."

"Jesus H. Christ!" Gorson remarked.

"He'd walk," Joe muttered as he lowered his binoculars and turned. Lilly had come on deck and was setting up yet another weapon on a tripod.

"Cool it!" Joe snarled. "Haven't you started enough wars?"

The security man turned with an air of pained innocence. "You expect me to zap somebody with a parabolic mike?" he asked.

Lilly attached a half-meter dish with a microphone at the focal point to the tripod. Another famous first, Joe thought wryly. The security man was preparing to do the first longdistance eavesdropping.

He jacked the microphone into an amplifier and began aiming the parabolic dish. The swash of water and wind emerged from a speaker, a creak of complaining timbers and the groan of a loose socketed mast moving slightly with each wave. Then Joe heard the confused mutter of voices. The language had a vaguely German sound.

There was an abrupt exclamation as the man at the steering oar sighted the *Alice*. He yelled something and Joe waited to see if the other ship would attack or avoid. It did neither. Someone began clanging on a gong.

"Start engines?" Rose asked. "If that's general quarters—"

"Be ready." Joe wanted to slip away in the fog but he saw no great excitement aboard the grain ship. The clang settled into a regular tolling and abruptly Joe knew it was some ancient analogue to a foghorn. If they were where Lilly thought they were, perhaps there was reasonable security and the freighter would not worry about pirates. But surely the *Alice* would attract attention. Joe tried to remember if any ancient ships had carried more than one mast. He suspected they had not. Then he remembered that the *Alice* had only one mast since that tug and barge had broken her mizzen. The grain ship sailed steadily across the *Alice's* bows and began to disappear in the fog. "Hard over," Joe said, "Let's get out of here."

"Wait a minute," Lilly protested. "I'm trying to listen."

"Listen to them." Joe pointed at the second sail which was heading straight for the *Alice*. There was a rattlesnap of canvas as the ketch came about and headed blindly off into the fog on the opposite tack. Joe stuck his head below and saw Freedy hunched over the radar, glasses once more sliding down his nose. He posted an extra lookout in the bow just in case. "Keep your distance of everything and everybody," he told Gorson and went below.

An hour later Joe and Dr. Lilly clung to a raft too small to support either one of them.

Chapter 14

"How," Joe asked himself, "do I get into situations like this?"

"Because you swore to protect the constitution against all enemies, both foreign and domestic." Dr. Lilly clung to the same raft, which had been cobbled up from the broken stump of the mizzen and a few other bits of timber trimmed as Rose struggled to repair the mast. "You *are* agreed that we do less violence to the fabric of time by injecting only ourselves instead of a whole shipload of strange technology into this era?" the security man pursued.

Joe had agreed. And now the *Alice* was in the middle of next week sailing in circles and, according to the man who had it 'all worked out', would pick up him and Joe when their mission was finished.

Joe had argued, had protested, and had abruptly found himself going along. He hadn't wanted to. All he wanted was to stay aboard the *Alice* and keep his people together and remember that he was getting old and stiff for this kind of shenanigans. He suspected that Dr. Lilly had not really wanted him along either. Perhaps the good doctor knew what

Joe was planning and knew that unless Joe went along too there would be no *Alice* waiting to pluck him from the jaws of vengeance once he had done whatever nastiness he came here to do.

Joe looked away from Lilly and wondered if Gorson would follow orders. Joe had been explicit. "Don't come back for either one of us," he had told the chief.

"But Joe!"

"No. You're in charge. Take care of things and—don't throw Dr. Greybull overboard. He doesn't seem to be such a bad guy."

"But Joe—"

"Take care of Margaret," Joe said. "Or I'll haunt you."

"But can't we just—"

"I'm afraid not," Joe said. "He'll outmaneuver us somehow. But I don't think he's expecting me to be a throwaway too."

"There's got to be a way."

"There is. This is it."

The chief had suddenly turned away in the darkness. "I'll do it," he had promised in a strange, gruff voice.

So now Joe clung to a raft with his fellow waif, praying Lilly would not work it out too soon.

"No funny business with hidden weapons either," Joe had insisted.

"Not even a knife?" Lilly asked.

"I mean technology out of this era. We'll have to defend ourselves somehow."

"Against what?" Lilly asked.

Joe tried to remember how many miles north of the shark-infested mouths of the Nile they were. Not far enough. "Against everybody," he said. "What do you suppose happened to POWs or shipwrecked strangers in these times? They had to recruit galley slaves from somewhere."

"The same happens in Siberia in our times," Lilly said. "It depends on who rescues them." He spat as a wavelet filled his mouth with brine. "Cool it. I hear them."

Joe pumped water from his ears and tried to listen. Somewhere off in the fog a gong clanged. The sound seemed slightly louder now.

"Don't speak English," Lilly warned in a low voice.

"Why not? Shipwrecked sailors could speak some unknown local dialect." Joe paused and added, "It's not as if somebody was going to understand us a thousand years before English was invented."

Lilly had agonized over what this era's style in facial adornment might be. Joe could not enlighten him beyond reminding the weapons man that, though Romans had shaved one century and worn beards the next, they had always insisted that only some trousered northern barbarian would wear a mustache without a beard. Lilly seemed shorn and inoffensive without his. He focussed laser eyes on Joe. "One word in any modern language scrubs this mission and us." He began yelling.

To Joe's surprise he still recognized the words even after the long hiatus in his studies. He clung to the raft and waited, wishing the water was warmer. The *Alice* was gone off into wherever she went in a time jump and . . . This water demanded a wet suit and all he had was the baggy *himation* that Lilly had produced as part of their disguise. He began shivering.

"*Pou isai?*" a voice shouted.

"Over here! This way!" Lilly renewed his shouting and moments later the bow of the freighter emerged from the fog. A lookout barked a single word and the helmsman turned until the square sail spilled wind. Joe recalled the last time he had gone aboard a strange vessel. He had ended up pulling a galley oar. But another ten minutes in this water would kill him even sooner. He got around to the other side of the raft with Lilly and they began kicking toward the hove-to-freighter.

The lookout in the bows was a young man with short sandy hair. He tossed a rope end. While Joe struggled to climb aboard Lilly's hands were busy underwater. There was a sudden 'thunk' and planking in the freighter's bow shuddered. The man pulling Joe aboard glanced curiously over the side. A moment later Lilly was aboard, once more suffused with that same aura of suppressed triumph as just before the patrol boat blew up. Joe gave the weapons man a long look.

Lilly grinned, then turned to the man who had helped them aboard. *"Ef charisto,"* he said.

Joe added his eucharist to Lilly's thanks and they sprawled on the deck, hawking and spitting somewhat more salt water than they had actually swallowed. "Did you plant a limpet mine?" Joe hissed when their rescuer trotted aft.

"Okhi!" Lilly shook his head and glared.

Joe sighed and struggled to remember his Greek. There was nothing ambiguous about the weapons man's 'no'. Whatever he had done, Joe knew he would sooner or later find out—and that he was not going to like it. He was still shivering from their thirty minute soak.

Lilly pulled his *himation* over his head. Sitting naked, he began matter of factly wringing water from the garment. Joe noted idly that neither he nor the weapons man had been mutilated for reasons religious or sanitary. They could pass for Greeks—unless those aboard the ship were really Greek. What difference did it make? Lilly's fluent *koine* was the English of its day, spoken by everyone who had to communicate with strangers.

A middle aged man in impressive purplish brown robes that Joe suspected were not proper sailor garb stood over them. "Where from and where bound for?" He seemed deliberately to be speaking a simplified pidgin.

Joe thought furiously, realizing that he still had no real proof that Lilly's opinion was correct. To have sailed from some Mediterranean port would be difficult to explain if they happened now to be in the landlocked Caspian or somesuch unlikely place.

Before Joe could invent a reply the weapons man was off and running. His *koine* was too fast but Joe caught *Skandariya* which had to be Alexandria. He struggled to attune his ears, and learned that they had been blown off course and had no slightest idea where they were but that the *Damietta Isis* with a mixed cargo had been bound for Konstantinopolis.

Joe felt an abrupt hand on the back of his neck. It was Lilly forcing him face down on the deck.

"Master!" The weapons man was grovelling. "Our lives are yours. Do with us what thou wilt."

Was there no end of surprises in this mercurial doctor? Joe suppressed the disgust that flooded him. Lilly was absolutely right for this time and place. If Joe had been capable of a little more humility would it have kept him from the galleys? He added his supplications to those of the weapons man.

"Enough," the swarthy man said. "Let me have a look at you."

They stood. Lilly had been wringing out his *himation* and was naked. Joe still shivered in his.

"You may call me Theodore," Their new owner had dropped the simplified pidgin. His Greek was different from any Joe had ever learned. His *f*'s, his *v*'s and *b*'s all melded into the same indeterminate sound until even his *Theodore* seemed to begin with something midway between an English *th* and a Greek *ph*. "And what do I call you two?" he added.

"My old name, lord, is difficult to say but since I came to the true faith I too am an adorer of God," Lilly spoke in the same fulsome accents. "I am baptized Dorotheo." Turning, he added, "And my tongue-afflicted fellow server of the one true God is Joseph."

"Can Joseph not understand that one does not judge a horse by his saddle?"

Joe took the hint and removed his soaked *himation*. From the corner of his eye he saw a young woman watching with idle curiosity from the afterdeck.

While Theodore studied the warm bodies in front of him Joe studied for some glint of his new owner's interest. He concluded that Theodore was probably not 'that way'. Satisfied that they were in reasonable health, the swarthy man said, "I'm something of a stranger in these parts myself. Does everyone wear short hair and shave like you two?"

"Only scholars, my lord," Lilly had an answer for everything. Joe wondered how much the weapons man was mak-

ing up. If they lived long enough to make it ashore any
fabrication was sure to backfire.

"You are scholars?"

"Of very modest attainments, my lord," Lilly flattered.
"Apart from my own barbarous tongue I know Latin and
Greek. Joseph also has some knowledge of these tongues."

"Can you count?"

Lilly was confused. "In what language?"

"Yes, my lord," Joe hastened. "We have a secret way to
prevent error and theft. A way," he added, "which also is a
holy mystery to tax collectors." There was an abrupt glint of
interest in Theodore's dark eyes. While Lilly glowered Joe
hinted at future developments in creative bookkeeping. "If
you anticipate any problems entering port we can get right to
work."

Even though they sat crosslegged and alone in their own
sheltered corner of the afterdeck Lilly was still careful to
speak only in Greek as they struggled to decipher blotted
entries on a parchment roll that threatened to disintegrate in
the damp air.

Joe had given up and framed his replies in Latin which was
easier for him. "So we're not in the Mediterranean," he
conceded. "If we're in the Dardanelles no wonder there's so
much traffic." Circling in these foggy straits, the *Alice* was
probably aground by now.

"Not the Dardanelles," Lilly said. "Not if we're to be in
port tomorrow."

Joe he supposed Istanbul, Constaninople, Byzantium—
whatever they called that polynomial city in this century—
would be where they tied up. Meanwhile, where was the
Alice? Was Gorson taking care of things or was he up to his
old tricks? Was Margaret taking care of herself?

"Didn't take you *spurii* long to find a home, did it?" It
was the short sandy haired man who had rescued them. His
himation, bloused up above his knees, gave the sailor the
topheavy look of a pouter pigeon.

"Bastard yourself," Joe replied. "It takes one to know one." Abruptly he realized they were both speaking Latin.

"Where you from?"

"We sailed from Alexandria—" Lilly began.

"That's not the question I asked."

"Our land is far," Joe began. "Our village is tiny. Few people in the great world have ever heard of it."

"Try me."

Joe almost said America. Then he remembered Lilly's warning.

"Hibernia," Lilly said with a hint of a grin.

The weapons man's grin disappeared when the sailor said something of which Joe only caught what sounded like *Erin*.

"*Faex taurina*," the sailor said and walked off with a grin of his own. Joe suspected that 'bullshit' did not translate directly into 3rd century Latin no matter what the young man's usage. He looked at Lilly who was looking at the sailor's back. Finally the weapons man returned to their parchment and jumbled accounts.

The wind freshened and abruptly the fog was gone. The land was too far to make out anything but an hour later Joe saw the outlines of a considerable town. He realized with a sudden pang that in spite of his adventures years ago, this was the first time he had ever actually come close to a real city of antiquity.

"Konstantinopolis." Their owner had appeared from nowhere and stood behind them. "You've been there, of course."

"Not lately," Joe admitted.

An hour later the *Sancta Chrisma* was closer to the teeming oriental mélange of elegance and squalor. As the shores of Europe and Asia drew together Joe began to pick out individual buildings. It was not his era and he knew little of what to expect. By the 3rd century A.D. Rome had some respectable antiquities of its own. But Byzantium . . . Even though there had been a city on the New Rome site a millenium before Old Rome was founded, Joe wasn't even sure if this unzoned mix of palace and pigeon hole had a sewer system. He was afraid to ask about something that was probably common knowledge in this era.

As the ship moved eastward in the light air the Sea of Marmara pinched into the Bosphorus. Joe scanned the left shore, searching for the outlines of St. Sophia's.

"Over there," Lilly was saying to Theodore, "looks like a nice spot for a cathedral." The weapons man shot a glance of swift amusement at Joe, who suddenly remembered that if they were when Lilly thought they were, Justinian's monument to Holy Wisdom would not be built for another 3-½ centuries. "Doesn't look like the last time I was here," Lilly added with an air of transparent puzzlement.

"You've been here before then?" Theodore asked.

"Often, my lord. But the palace . . ."

Joe understood then that Lilly had no idea of the city's present layout. He was slyly interrogating their new master.

Abruptly the ship sheered off astarboard toward the Asiatic shore. Joe contained his disappointment at not getting a look at Constantinople's celebrated Golden Horn but they were heading for the docks at Scutari, which the Turks in another 1100 years would come to call Uskudar.

"My lord goes to the council then?" Lilly said.

Theodore gave them a sharp glance, then relaxed. "It would seem," he said drily, "that you can take the bishop out of the robes but you cannot take the robes out of the bishop."

Joe felt wheels spin. Those people in Washington hadn't been kidding. Somebody had gone to more care than Joe had believed possible to arrange this series of coincidences. He caught a flicker of Lilly's mocking grin.

A half hour later Joe and Lilly were telling pious falsehoods to an unimpressed customs agent.

"Look," that dyspeptic man said tiredly, "I understand that your master Theodore is here on official business. He's not the first come here to confer with other bishops at the specific request of his Imperial Majesty, Caesar et Imperator Constantinus."

"But—" Joe protested.

"I also realize that it's only natural that the bishop bring enough merchandise to finance his stay, that there's no profit motive in your voyage but . . .

One of these days Joe was going to have to look into the history of foreign exchange. He knew the world's first vending machine had sold holy water but who invented the credit card?

"What you pious pinheads can't seem to get through your livers," the customs man continued, "is that neither emperors nor customs inspectors can continue in their appointed rounds without an assured cash flow—and that the deficit is not coming out of my hide."

Theodore put an abrupt end to the discussion. Putting aside the elegantly carved and inlaid crozier that had not left his hands since they raised port, the bishop raised his hands in an ecclesiastical blessing. He passed them over the customs man's head in a gesture that ended with a single gold *solidus*. Cargo began moving onto the dock where several buyers and a throng of human pack animals lounged, the *hamals'* heads pillowed on their pack saddles. To Joe it seemed that Bishop Theodore had managed well enough without his new accountants. Lilly's grin was less certain.

The cargo was offloaded and manifests checked off with no more than the usual bungles. Late in the afternoon a smiling one-eyed man in short jerkin and a kilt-and-leggins device midway between a Scotsman and a Greek *evzon* appeared. He handed over a pouch to Theodore who dumped it on deck and counted more gold *solidi* than he had gotten from all the other buyers put together. "Farewell, thou cranky illsteering bucket!" Bishop Theodore's Christian love apparently did not extend to the *Sancta Chrisma*.

The bishop surveyed his two new accountants doubtfully then, leaning on his crozier, sent off a crewman. It was the same sandy haired man who had spoken of taurine feces. Abruptly Joe remembered that the proper word was *stercus*. Or was it? He wasn't familiar with 3rd century slang.

They were bundling up to leave. Joe looked for Lilly and

felt an instant of panic at the realization that the weapons man had slipped away. Joe was telling himself he was better off without that trigger happy berserker when the security expert came back off the dock with a bulge in his bulky *himation*. Lilly's hair was wet. Now Joe knew he had fastened something underwater outside the ship's bow.

The bulge was nearly invisible in the salt stiffened wrinkles of Lilly's garment. The sandy haired Latin speaker returned with a guide and two athletic sheep. The ship's company formed up to march off inland.

Theodore seemed in some haste and Joe wondered if his ship had been delayed. They marched into gathering darkness. Joe and Lilly each bore a sack of the bishop's earthly possessions. Joe's neck and shoulders began complaining. He stumbled. *I'm too old for this kind of crap*.

When would he see the *Alice* again? Margaret? Joe had a foreboding that, like Raquel, he would end up marooned in some wrong place and time and would never view home again. From the darkness of a stony path on the Asiatic side of the Bosphorus the Imperial Presidency didn't seem all that bad.

Then abruptly the procession halted after no more than three or four kilometers. They had quitted the fleshpots of Scutari and were within the low walls of a caravanserai which offered some security. Abruptly Joe recalled the young woman he had seen aboard the *Sancta Chrisma*. The freighter had not been large enough to lose somebody. What had happened to her?

The bishop's men were setting up camp with practiced efficiency. Joe tried to make himself useful and only got in the way. Bishop Theodore and his crozier were nowhere to be seen. Off saying his evening mass, Joe suspected.

One man cut a sheep's throat and had the unhappy animal skinned before it stopped bleating. The butcher removed the animal's innards carefully, slitting open the stomach and saving its contents. He squeezed still-squirming intestines between thumb and forefinger, then held out their lower end while his helper poured from an amphora. When water emerged reasonably clear from the small intestine the butcher put the anus to his mouth and blew. Water sprayed from his pump-and-hose to rinse the carcass clean. They spitted the sheep on a rack to one side of the fire and Joe realized it would be hours before anyone ate. Which didn't matter. There was a tremendous ground swell abuilding in Joe's stomach as he and Lilly stayed back and strove not to make waves.

The rest of the party gathered about the fire and waited for a stomach-contents-plus-liver-and-kidneys stew to boil. When it did nobody called Joe or Lilly to eat. To Joe's queasy satisfaction Lilly did not seem hungry either. They lounged away from the fire, wondering when the bishop would reappear.

He did not.

Instead, the young sandy haired man finished eating and moved away from the fire, suddenly flanked by the other six. "Well now isn't this cozy," Sandy Hair said. "Just the bunch of us here all alone."

Chapter 15

Joe sighed. He should have realized this was going to happen when a pair of strangers were plucked from the sea and immediately plopped into a job that the bishop's permanent retainers must have intrigued for. One of these men had probably been the bookkeeper.

"In medio?" Lilly muttered. *"Ego ad extremos."*

Lilly had switched languages, assuming that even if the bishop's men all knew Greek, some would not speak Latin.

Joe did not care to plunge into the middle of the lineup even if Lilly did think he could take care of both ends. "What can we do to soothe your good Christian souls—?" he began.

"Gloria Deo in excelsis!" Lilly charged.

Other choices eliminated, Joe added a *"Pro Deo et patria!"* as he drove his shoulder into the midsection of the sandy haired man who had pulled him aboard. There was a whoosh of escaping air, followed by an eruption of the mutton-and-stomach-contents of still another stomach. Joe spun and clipped another man who had not yet gotten turned around.

Lilly's arms spun like windmills in the firelight as he distributed karate chops to startled men who still strove to settle into the formalized stance of Graeco-Roman wrestling. Three were on the ground. One had sense enough to run. Showing more white of eye than was strictly necessary, the others tried to surround Lilly and Joe.

"Totally unchristian," Lilly was saying as he feinted toward one, then drove his first sideways into the wide open midsection of another. The man around the midsection abruptly stopped trying to grapple. "No brotherly love at all," Lilly complained. "A lamentable lack of *philadelphia*."

"Pittsburgh too," Joe muttered as he clobbered a man trying to climb Lilly's back.

"*Irene*", the last man gasped as Joe and Lilly began closing in.

"Peace?" Lilly mocked. "From the butcher's blade?"

Abruptly Joe remembered how the sheep had died. And Lilly, without a second thought, had charged barehanded . . .

"You could have originated the peace and prevented all this," Lilly was saying. "The outcome clearly demonstrates that the good bishop's men stand not well in the eyes of God."

Or uninstructed in the next 15 centuries' progress in the art of mayhem.

The bishop's sole remaining combatant had survived other brawls in this unruly era. He had availed himself of the proper spells against sorcery or other improper influences. But to be hit suddenly with a too-plausible explanation of Lilly's superior version of Christian love was too much. The knife he was hiding dropped from a nerveless hand.

Lilly gave the wretch two fat ears. "To impress upon you the value of peace," he said, "and because I don't have a boat hook to give you my kind of headache." He inventoried six survivors. "Linger unshriven in outer darkness," he shouted and Joe remembered a seventh man who had run.

While the others licked their wounds Joe and Lilly went to the fire and tore chunks from the roasting sheep. They were eating when Joe looked up into Theodore's thoughtful eyes. In the shadows beside the bishop was a shorter heavily robed figure.

"Master!" Lilly declaimed. "God lengthen thy days and lead thy flock in the paths of righteousness."

"It looks as if you'd already pointed them in the proper direction," Theodore said. "I hope you'll leave a little of that for my niece and me."

Joe hastened to make room by the fire. The bishop lowered himself carefully with his shepherd's crook shaped crozier and sat. "Beloved brethren," Joe snapped. "Some service for our lord." As the bishop's battered retainers made themselves busy Joe had time to realize that Theodore's absence had not been accidental. The bishop would have known that pecking orders had to be reestablished. Like any good commander, he had absented himself and let nature take its course. It was less easy for Joe to guess whether the bishop could have predicted the outcome.

"Unusual to find scholars who are also men-at-arms," the bishop said.

"My lord," Lilly declaimed, "Our modest attainments seemed unfitting of mention."

"Thus spake the young David." Bishop Theodore seemed to be enjoying himself thoroughly.

Joe considered possible reasons and found each deficient. He followed Lilly's fawning lead and they struggled to outdo one another in making the bishop and his niece comfortable.

"Thy men, my lord, have honorable attainments," Lilly said. "They must be of the land whence thy magnificent crozier since they all speak Latin."

"First I've heard of it," Theodore said. "Kormyches dwelt for a time in Italy but the others have naught but koine and their own barbarous tongues."

Kormyches . . . ? *Cormac!* The sandy haired Irishman who had pulled them aboard. Joe decided he was going to have to brush up on Lilly's form of interrogation.

Though there was no way to see inside the voluminous robes she wore against the night air Joe suspected the bishop's niece might be quite young. He caught Lilly's speculative glance and wondered what new trouble the weapons man would get him into. Grudgingly, Joe knew Lilly's had been the only solution unless they resigned themselves to sucking hind tit for the remainder of their stay with the Right Reverend Father in God, Theodore.

The bishop set watches. The bishop's men rummaged in their bundles and settled down for the night. Lilly appropriated the single untouched pack. With a grin, he scooted close to Joe and they lay back-to-back. "Only one sane man in the lot," Lilly said cheerfully. "And he dwelleth in the outer darkness while we share his cloak."

There was something wrong with Lilly's argument. Joe knew it. But he had still not found the hole when he fell asleep.

He awoke to the sudden realization that he and Lilly were not the cloak's only occupants. Scratching, he sensed that Lilly was also awake, listening. What had happened to the lookout who was supposed to keep the fire burning? *"Kyrie'mou!"* someone was whispering.

"Ti symvenia?" Lilly's whisper was just as low.

"My lord," the whisper repeated, "Strangers come. Evil men I think."

The whisperer was the wretch run off into the darkness, and whose cloak he and Lilly shared.

"Strangers come and stranger ones go," Lilly murmured. He poked a hand at Joe. The hand held a knife. Joe wanted to consult but the weapons man had already slithered off.

Joe crouched in the darkness. *What am I doing here?* He had asked the same question before and never gotten a satisfactory reply. Struggling to ignore the bonechilling cold he wrapped the cloak around his left forearm and hefted the knife.

One of the bishop's men seemed afflicted with apnea, not breathing for half a minute at a time, then gulping air at one death rattle's distance from eternity. The racket nearly drowned out the others' snores. Joe began scooting away

from where they had been sleeping. Away from the dead
campfire he could hear tiny rustles of foraging roach and
rodent. No matter how he strained his ears, he could hear
nothing else.

There was a sudden rustling thump as something heavy hit
ground. Joe rotated his head slowly, trying to zero in on the
sound. The thump was followed by an odd whistle that
almost became words before it settled into a bubbling gurgle.

Joe stood very still holding his breath as he listened.
Slowly he began turning again and caught a faint silhouette.
He was raising the knife when he realized it was Lilly—his
silhouette very different without his huge mustache.

"Brother Joseph!" Lilly came oozing out of the darkness.

Joe squinted. The weapons man was cleaning his knife
with a hank of grass. "Only one?" Joe whispered.

"Three. The others—lost heart." Lilly was composing
himself to sleep again.

"Kyrie' mou!"

"Go tell Kormyches to give you his cloak," Lilly said,
"and for him to get the fire going and stand a proper guard if
he hopes to prolong his owed-me life."

Joe decided not to pester the weapons man with questions.
He scooted against Lilly's back and, after a thoughtful hour,
shivered himself to sleep.

Someone found three bodies next morning while Joe and
Lilly were having a refreshing Roman breakfast of cold water
with enough wine to give it a faint pinkish tinge. Two had
bruised throats and, probably, fractured hyoid bones, which
explained why they had not made vocal objection to the holes
in their chests. The third victim's life had flowed noisily out
of his throat to discourage any still-hidden raiders. "Just
bandits, I suppose," Joe ventured. He could not recall when
last he had felt so ineffectual.

Lilly gave him that controlled grin. "Or an effort to
influence the voting."

"I still don't know the good guys from the bad guys," Joe
complained.

"You'll find out soon."

"Are we close? I was wondering why the bishop didn't sail directly there."

"Nicaea's not a seaport," Lilly said. "It's on Lake Ascania. *Eis Nikaian* was the emperor's summer palace: close to the big city, the port, and the major transport routes."

A flashlightsized bulb glimmered above Joe's head. "Iznik?"

Lilly glanced around. "Someday it will be," he said, "When the Eastern Empire falls and some nomadic Turkish tribe cannot pronounce the Greek."

Joe nodded. "But that's a hundred mile walk. We should have sailed down the coast to Gemlik."

"Port-of-entry," Lilly guessed. "Or maybe the old boy knew he couldn't sell his ship or cargo in a small town."

"I still don't know what we're supposed to do," Joe protested. "Whom do we back?"

"The Arians."

"But they let the wild Germans resurrect all their local spooks and turn them into saints and—"

"Only later," Lilly said. "As of now monotheistic Arianism is strong in the East. If Athanasius wins we're stuck with the Trinity and the Islamic reaction becomes inevitable."

"Monotheistic? With all those—"

"So the son of God loses a capital letter and becomes one more lower case god, for which read saint or prophet or whatever. It removes the single obstacle that kept Islam and Christianity separated."

"I wonder what St. Ignatius and all those old Moorkillers would have to say."

"I'm the Christian." Lilly studied Joe and grinned. "All hogwash and superstition," he added. "Why should it bother you?"

After last night no one suggested that Joe or Lilly share in the work or bear any burdens. The bishop's men struck camp and they began walking, still accompanied by Theodore's unseen niece in her allencompassing robes.

The country was green and lush, not at all like Joe's few

glimpses of the near east. From the fresh grass and new growths of sage and fennel, he decided it must be spring.

Instead of walking inland the bishop directed them back toward the coast where all hands crowded aboard a somewhat smaller boat crewed by lean hardfaced men who doubled at oars when wind and current conspired against them. Thirty hours later the bishop doled out coins to a skipper whose plans to rob and deep-six them had been foiled by Joe and Lilly's oily smiles as they whetted daggers.

Walking inland from Gemlik Joe discovered that infantrymen really can march and sleep at the same time. He came into awareness only as they approached the double line of Roman walls that surrounded Nicaea. The city was divided into four nearly equal quarters by twin main streets that led from gates in each wall and crossed at the city center. In the square was a large statue which Joe did not recognize.

He wondered if the biship would have a *hospes* relationship with some local citizen or if they were condemned to lodge in a *caupona* open to the fleabitten public. Not that it made that much difference after a night under somebody else's robe. Joe scratched and tried to memorize the layout of the town.

It was a busy place, full of porters and pack animals bearing loads that nearly hid them. Water vendors offered brass cupsful with shrill cries. Brass pot urinals on every corner collected the necessary caustic for the fullers trade. Black cloaked men bore oddshaped buckets that mystified Joe until a citizen with an urgent need handed one an *obolos*. While the citizen squatted astraddle the bucket the bearer held the cloak around him.

An hour later the bishop's party were lodged in the outbuildings of the townhouse of what Joe thought was a Deacon Eumolpida. The surname sent a faint tremor of alarm through Joe. No big deal, he decided. A man of this era was no more likely to take hereditary priesthood any more seriously than a modernday Cohen.

"I hope to holy Mahan there's time to get some sleep," Joe grumbled.

"Pray not to unknown gods!" Lilly warned.

Joe was about to ask him what difference it made when nobody here could understand English. He contained himself abruptly as Theodore appeared. "You two get some rest right now," the bishop instructed.

"It shall be done, my lord," Lilly said.

"I want the pair of you fresh to watch my back," Theodore continued. "Tomorrow we go to the council."

Joe caught the hint of triumph in Lilly's air and once more wondered just how Washington could have worked it all out this neatly. He was still wondering when sleep overcame his burning feet.

Chapter 16

The Eumolpidae house was uncomplicated by any heating system. Joe awoke as a harelipped girl entered their mud-brick chamber with a brazier capable of warming one hand or foot at a time. *"Kalli mera,"* he greeted, "And what's your name?"

The girl gave Joe the look one gets from someone who's been raped by friendly strangers before. She scuttled backward out of the room.

Lilly laughed. "Doesn't augur well for room service." He ran a finger over his gums and spat water out the window. "How you fixed for blades?" His good humor evaporated at the sound of someone walking across the atrium. Joe whetted the knife Lilly had given him on the stone of their threshold and managed after a time to remove some of the more bothersome hairs around his mouth. The girl returned with round, hamburger-bunsized loaves of hot brown bread and a fresh ewer of water.

Lilly laid some blarney on her and got the ghost of a harelipped smile but the girl was careful to keep herself beyond grabbing distance as she scooted once more out the door.

The weapons man turned to Joe. "Did you happen to notice which way the john is?"

"About thirteen hundred years thataway."

"But in a city—in a house as elegant as this—"

Joe shrugged. "When in Rome."

"This isn't Rome."

"It's 3rd century Roman Empire culture."

"I don't want to make myself conspicuous asking the wrong questions," Lilly said.

"Step out into the atrium and follow your nose."

Lilly gave him a fishy look and opened the door. "I can't smell anything except cooking."

"You're on the right track." Joe saw the weapons man's disbelief and shrugged. "Follow me," he said. To the first servant who bustled across the atrium he added a hasty, "Where's the kitchen?"

The man with a pair of bedrolls on his back pointed toward the front of the house.

Joe led a doubting Lilly into the room where a dozen men and women were busy with the chores of an age when milk came to the door in its original container and was milked into the customer's pitcher.

There was a loud thwap-splash as Lilly entered. He grabbed for his knife in the instant before he saw a hare's intestines land in the gutter that traversed an inclined, stone flagged floor. Water flowed from an ovalshaped lead pipe in one wall and ran across the room, out through the wall that faced the street. At this street end of the gutter an old woman squatted. "*Kalli mera*," Joe greeted and straddled the gutter just upstream. Vegetable parings, guts and an occasional fishhead passed beneath him out into the opensewered street.

"When in Rome," Lilly said through gritted teeth. The kitchen help paid him not the slightest attention. "Takes a little getting used to," the weapons man admitted as they made it back to their room.

"You know the language well enough," Joe said. "Didn't the good Jesuits ever explain to you that this is a time when the finest gentleman in the most elegant company didn't hesitate to yell for the pisspot right in the middle of dinner?"

Lilly gave him a green look, then suddenly grinned. "Funny how the mind filters out little things like that," he mused.

The harelipped girl appeared again. This time she beckoned.

Bishop Theodore was in what Joe assumed was full regalia for a bishop: a hightopped mitre, purple robes, and bearing his magnificently inlaid crozier. Considerably more impressive than aboard ship, he aimed Joe and Lilly toward a room in the rear of the hollow-square house. Lilly surveyed the private armory and looked at the bishop. "Is anything forbidden—any weapon we should not take?" he asked.

The bishop thought a moment and shook his head. "I hope you weren't considering sorcery or any of the diabolical arts," he finally said.

"My lord, we are devout in our Christian belief," Lilly said stiffly. "But what awaits us?"

"Trouble."

The weapons man shrugged. "It's your life. We can don full armor and be ready to stand off a mob or an army. While we're putting on a show some quiet little widow with a knife amid her flowers kisses your ring, slips it in, and puts us out of a job."

"I had not thought of it that way," Theodore conceded. "I doubt if we'll have mobs or large scale attacks. But so many of my party have fallen victim to footpads that coincidence stretches unto breaking."

Joe was tempted to ask the bishop which party he belonged to but he suspected this would be an even greater gaffe than for Lilly to ask where the john.

Lilly thought a moment, then selected light armor and a seven foot spear.

"Very impressive," Joe grunted.

"Supposed to be. It's for you."

"Even if I knew how to use it that's the most impractical damned—"

"At first hint of trouble you shuck this window dressing and do the wellwhetted unexpected."

"Hope I can get it off in time," Joe grumbled. "What're you wearing?"

"Nothing. You're my stalking horse. I'll get a wax tablet and practice shorthand while I watch the bishop's back and yours." Lilly turned to Theodore. "Whenever my lord is ready—"

As they walked the streets of Nicaea toward the lakeshore palace Joe noted that hawkers of apples and olives and meat pasties did not pester the bishop or his attendants. He wondered if his appearance was too intimidating or if the hawkers merely knew that no one in robes of such magnificent winedark purple would ever condescend to street food.

Three blocks from Deacon Eumolpida's house an elderly man in robes very like Theodore's appeared with four attendants. The other bishop's crozier, Joe noted, was elegant enough but did not compare with Theodore's. Two of his attendants looked like clerks. Lilly studied Theodore for a clue but the old man gave a friendly wave and then he and Theodore were walking together and conversing in a Greek too swift and oddly accented for Joe. Joe and Lilly eyed the other bishop's men with the wary formality of dogs in strange territory.

The taller of the other bishop's men sized up Lilly as a pencil pusher and turned to Joe whose armor gave him the look of a fellow fighting man. "First day here?" He and the other redhaired man had an Irish look. Their short swords were Roman.

Joe nodded. "Been much trouble?"

"So far," the tall man said, "they're all talking Christian love."

"When'd the council start?" Joe asked.

"Hasn't really started yet," the longlipped man said. "People keep drifting in. Maybe today."

Lilly smiled a secret little smile. "Once the emperor gets down to business—"

The redhaired man-at-arms gave him an odd look. "Not much chance of him wasting time down here. He just called all the old bastards in and said if they want Christianity to be the official religion they better get their act together and decide just what it is."

"I suppose Athanasius is here—?" Lilly guessed.

"Bigger than life and twice as nasty." The man-at-arms made sure the two bishops were not listening and then added, "I ain't no philosopher but devil take me if I can make anus from esophagus out of that father-son-holy ghost crap. Which side you guys on?"

Joe suspected any answer would be wrong. Lilly passed it off with a shrug. "Whatever the old man says." He nodded at Theodore's purple robed back.

"Master! Nice strong boy?"

Joe tried to ignore the salesman. The flesh peddler studied them doubtfully, unsure what strange tastes might turn on foreigners. "Girls too," he added.

"I prepare for thee a place in hell," Joe said, and encouraged the peddler's departure with the point of his spear. The breastplate was heavy and the shoulder straps were already chafing under the cloak he wore. His head and neck ached from the unaccustomed weight of the helmet whose huge plume tried to drag him alee with the slightest puff of breeze. The morning was still chilly but there was a hint of heat to come.

Joe eyed his spear. It was a foot longer than he and, impressive as it might be, Joe knew the little man he had chased away could have grabbed it easily and used it to beat him severely about the head and shoulders.

How had he let Lilly inveigle him into this? Forty-eight hours ago he had been sorting out ways to kill the man who now fawned on Bishop Theodore, pretending to take down his every word on a piece of board smeared with wax which Lilly was constantly smoothing out with the spoonshaped 'eraser' on the opposite end of his stylus. Joe was thinking dire thoughts of Margaret alone with all those studs aboard the *Alice* when abruptly he realized they had reached the palace gates.

Bishop Theodore and his party were passed by the palace guard and a moment later Joe found himself in— He had not really known what to expect. Somewhere, he supposed, the emperor's summer palace would have private quarters but this huge vaulted room was some kind of audience hall. At one end of the rectangular chamber was a small trestle table with four *cathedra* armchairs behind it. The remainder of the frigid granite and marble chamber was bare of furniture.

This was, Joe reflected, a cut more primitive than the barewall accomodation of a medieval cathedral where the censer's ritual smoke's more practical purpose was to drown out the odor of Christians just in from the provinces and camped out on the cathedral floor.

Here in the emperor's summer palace each bishop's party had staked out a piece of bare floor. Men-at-arms guarded their minuscule borders with the jealous zeal of penguins at a rookery. Down the center of the chamber was a yardwide division.

Joe wondered if the split divided hostile parties or was merely kept open so the *cathedra* could be approached. He turned to see on which side of the aisle Bishop Theodore wanted to stake his claim. Theodore and Lilly were edging toward the left.

There was still space toward the rear of the hall. Joe was relieved when the bishop did not demand that they force room for him up front. It struck him that both Theodore and his bishop friend met on the street were singularly tranquil for men under threat of assassination. Perhaps they took their Christianity seriously. They took up adjoining territory and folded shawls to create some hint of softness on the marble floor.

An hour later Joe knew why Lilly had selected the spear for him. It was handy to lean on.

Lilly sat crosslegged, listening to his master and the other bishop, taking an occasional note and spending much of his time smoothing out the wax of his tablet with the spoon-shaped end of the stylus which he warmed periodically over a teapot style lamp that smoked and stank of rancid olive oil. Abruptly there was a stir of attention. *"Ave imperator!"* somebody shouted.

As all hands scrambled to their feet and raised fists in a prehitlerian salute Joe felt a sudden *frisson*. The other man-at-arms had been wrong about the emperor coming. After all his piddling about on the edges of history Joe had actually managed just this once to get into the center of events! That unimpressive man up there behind the table and the four *cathedra* chairs had to be Constantinus the Great.

Great if, for nothing else, he had overcome bastardy and English blood to make himself emperor. He had moved the capital—would move it next year Joe abruptly remembered—from a Rome no longer safe from barbarians to the ancient site of Byzantium which would become New Rome and would survive another millenium beyond the fall of the old Italian model.

The shouting quieted and Joe had time to study the elegant dandy in ecclesiastical garb who stood beside and slightly behind the emperor. This time the shouting came mostly from one side of the hall. The opposite side. He glanced at Lilly. Unheard in the shouting, the weapons expert carefully formed the words with his lips. After a couple of tries Joe understood that he was looking upon the creator of the Athanasian Creed. *How did Lilly know?* Then Joe realized the 'secretary' had been listening to the two bishops. Studying Athanasius and Emperor Konstantinos side by side Joe sensed that one of this pair had to be a snake oil salesman. The emperor did not look like a man who was selling anything.

Joe found himself dozing again, marveling at how his feet could ache in these flat sandals. But he was the man-at-arms. Which reminded him that he was supposed to be watching out for the bishop. Theodore sat on his folded shawl paying

close attention to some interminable argument about who
was to speak first. Finally, and with ill grace, Athanasius
seemed to surrender.

A thin, Arab-looking young man began speaking in high-
pitched Greek. Joe caught some reference to *homoousious*
but the hairsplitting theology was beyond him. Nobody
seemed to be threatening Bishop Theodore or anyone else
with violence. He wished he could sit down. Get a drink—
get out of this stinking and overcrowded chamber. God, it
was getting hot!

There was a sudden growl of outrage from Joe's side of the
hall. He didn't even know which side he was on. Abruptly
bishops were on their feet, shouting and brandishing fists in
most unchristian manner.

Up where the emperor, Athanasius, and two unidentified
men sat in the *cathedrae* the effect was the same. Athanasius
was on his feet, pointing a bony finger at the young man who
still ranted on about *homoousious*.

Bishop Theodore shot a quick glance and decided that Joe
was performing his bodyguard duties satisfactorily. He
began yelling too, with a singular lack of conviction. Joe
abruptly sensed that either Bishop Theodore knew the fix was
already in, or else the old man did not really give a damn who
won.

Joe glanced around on the off chance that someone could
be planning this moment to scrag Theodore. Nobody paid
them the slightest attention. Lilly struggled with his wax
tablet, pursing his lips as he rubbed with the spoonshaped end
of his stylus.

Joe glanced toward the front of the hall where the thin,
Arab-looking young man now thrust his own finger into
Athanasius's face. There was a faint 'psst' as something
whizzed past Joe's ear. He turned and Lilly was still struggling onehandedly with stylus and wax tablet while he
stowed something inside the bulky folds of his himation. Joe
glanced back toward the dais just in time to see the thin,
Arab-looking speaker collapse.

There was a moment of shocked silence. Athanasius stood

mouth ajar, his finger still pointing at the fallen debater. The silence grew. At its height a single voice roared *"Stryggos!"*

Theodore and his bishop friend spun. Joe knew that voice. Lilly's look of bland inquiry gave the two bishops a moment of uncertainty. It made little difference. Suddenly everybody on this side of the aisle had taken up the cry.

"Stryggos!" They were calling the author of the Athanasian creed a warlock.

While Bishop Athanasius stared at his still-pointing finger someone added 'evil eye' to his titles.

Chapter 17

Suddenly the summer palace was full of struggling men biting, kicking and slashing. Joe strained to keep some space around their party with a spear approximately six feet too long for these conditions.

"My lord," Lilly suggested, "Perhaps we should depart?"

Theodore and his bishop friend nodded. Each took a firm grip on his crozier. Joe thanked the immortal shade of Albert Thayer Mahan that they were in the rear, near the entrance of the hall. While other vicars of the Prince of Peace clawed toward the dais these two bishops' squads formed phalanx and began forcing their quiet way out.

Joe lost his helmet but managed to hang onto the spear, which was useless in these tight quarters. Lilly was working efficiently with knees and elbows. Though the unarmed 'secretary' never actually attacked anyone his stylus or the edge of his woodenbacked wax tablet seemed always to intersect with whatever chin came too close.

Finally they stood gasping in the palace courtyard. Joe had taken a truncheon just below his breastplate and was having trouble breathing but this was no place to rest. They hurried on toward the gate.

"What in hell's going on?" the guard demanded.

"They're holding an *agape*," Joe explained. "Might be a good idea if you turned out the guard before their love overwhelms the Emperor. One delegate's already been gathered to Abraham's bosom."

"Jesus Homoousos Christ!" the guard remarked, and began clanging a triangle.

"Didn't we agree not to bring modern weapons?'" Joe growled as he and Lilly stalked ahead of the bishops.

Lilly glanced over his shoulder. The other bishop's men-at-arms brought up the rear as they quickmarched away. The weather had changed since they had gone into the palace and there was a heavy hint of rain. "Who do you think that skinny fink was?" Lilly asked.

"The one you scragged with a silencer?"

"Not so loud! His name was Zenobius."

"Never heard of him!"

"Otherwise known as the bishop's 'niece'."

Joe stared. "The girl aboard ship?"

"Didn't your mother ever explain gender?"

"Even if she was a man, I never heard of him."

"In our time line you never will," Lilly said firmly. He paused. "Funny thing about Zenobius and several Greeks of our acquaintance. Ever notice how our Lord Bishop and Father in Christ, Theodore, seems to have trouble pronouncing his own name?"

"It's just some strange dialect."

Lilly glanced skyward. "Shit!" he muttered. "Rain's just what I need." He turned to face Joe. "What people have Greek names but can't pronounce a *theta*? Who transmogrifies Basil into Vassily, Eugene into Yevgeny, *Theodore into Fyodor*? Who inherited the Eastern Orthodox Chruch?"

Joe gave a quick glance over his shoulder at Bishop Theodore who moved with brisk assurance and talked more briskly with his friend in a patois too fast to follow. "We're working for a Russian?" Joe demanded.

"Working against him," Lilly corrected. "Now put a lid on it!"

The uproar from the summer palace was filtering into the rest of the city. Citizens divided themselves into the curious, who began swarming toward the source of the disturbance *vs.* the prudent who took in awnings and began barring the store fronts that occupied the ground floor of every house. The other bishop and his men did not split off as they approached Deacon Eumolpida's home.

Joe saw that this worried Lilly. He surveyed the weapons man with mixed feelings, knowing he would probably never escape this city without Lilly's help, yet hating the man whose solution to every problem was a silencer and a bullet.

Once inside the deacon's house Lilly took charge. Joe was amused at the change of attitude when the other bishop's men-at-arms discovered who Theodore's real security expert was. While Lilly posted guards and went about making the house secure Joe shucked heavy armor and leaned the spear in a corner of their room.

He knew this was not the end of it but he didn't know what else he could do at the moment. He stretched out on his pallet and tried to rest. There was a charged damp feel to the air. Joe wondered if a storm was coming. Unlike Lilly, he wished it would rain—anything to drown out the inevitable rioting. Was the *Alice* still sailing in circles out there somewhere? *Where was Margaret?*

The door opened. "Long day," Lilly observed, and stretched out on his pallet. Both eyes were black now from the Mexican boat hook but he had acquired no new lesions in today's affair. Joe looked at him apathetically. There was nothing to say. Either you accepted Lilly's way of doing things or—you killed him and thus became Lilly.

Joe tried to remember what he knew about the Council of Nicaea. He supposed it had been like any political process—replete with sordid little deals in back rooms. But he could not recall any major riots or assassinations. Surely the author of the Athanasian Creed had not been accused of witchcraft in Joe's time line. What would he be going home to?

Did he want to go?

The door opened again. Bishop Theodore leaned on his

crozier looking thoughtfully at them. "Don't get up," he said as Lilly commenced his usual fawning routine. "It's been a long day for all of us. He regarded his bodyguard with an infinite sadness. "You should not have done it," the bishop finally said.

"My lord?" Lilly began.

"It's done and will never be undone," the bishop said tiredly. "I should have known better than to trust Washington."

Very gradually it soaked into Joe's exhaustion that Bishop Theodore was speaking slightly accented English. He looked to Lilly who still lay relaxed on his pallet, gripping a silenced pistol. "Commies'll play hell getting Arab oil now," Lilly said, and flashed the grin that Joe had learned to dread.

Bishop Theodore-Fyodor shook his head. "You innocent!" he snapped. "*I* was working to restore the Tsar. Now we are all destroyed."

Joe stared at Lilly. "What were you working for?" he asked.

Lilly did not reply.

"Have you a means back to your own time?" Theodore asked.

"Don't you?" Lilly asked.

"Not closeby. Not that it matters when there's nothing to go back to." The bishop managed a hint of a smile. "But if I may quote from a more innocent time when our countries were on friendly terms, there'll be a hot time in the old town tonight."

There was another long pause while the bishop leaned on his crozier surveying them mournfully. "I was not the only one saw the sorcerer draw his pistol," he said. "My colleague Anastazy has been circulating your description. I do him, and perhaps humanity a disservice by warning you." Theodore sighed. "Too many people die in God's name." He was leaving the room when Lilly abruptly put down the pistol.

"My lord!" the weapons man wailed. "Bless me father, for I have sinned."

There was a hint of disgust in Bishop Fyodor. Then he pulled himself together and prepared to hear the Jesuit student's confession. Joe writhed in an agony of terminal embarrassment. Was this really happening. Was it some new ruse on Lilly's part? Lilly was on his knees, straining to kiss the bishop's crozier.

The weapons man jerked as if he had been shocked. There was a sudden whiff of ozone in the air. Lilly grinned in triumph as he wrested the crozier from the older man. Bishop Theodore gave a sad smile as he let go. There was a flash and the sound of a welding machine breaking arc. And then Dr. Lilly lay fibrillating on the floor. His hands were smoking.

"Forgive me," Theodore said to Joe, "but against violence what is an old man to do?" The stench of ozone discharge became stronger and as Fyodor fingered the crozier his robed form began to attenuate. Just before the bishop disappeared Joe thought he saw a wink.

Joe bent over the unconscious Lilly. He was trying to persuade himself to leave the weapons man to work it out for himself when he discovered a slight inaccuracy in Theodore's prophesy. Nicaea might be in for a hot time tonight but Joe was suddenly up to his neck in cold water.

He got an unexpected mouthful and learned it was fresh water. Beside him Lilly bobbed face down. Joe struggled to turn him over and keep him afloat. He knew immediately what had happened. This had happened once before when Howie had gotten himself detached from the *Alice* and abruptly found himself back aboard. They must have pulled off a time jump. Where and when would they be?

"Over here!" It was Gorson's hoarse voice. The chief stood in the bows as the *Alice* ghosted toward them. For an instant Joe was tempted to let himself sink.

"What in hell are you doing here?" Joe demanded. "You weren't supposed to come back."

Gorson jerked a thumb over his shoulder. In the rigging amidships Margaret White had slung a bos'n's chair and sat cradling an automatic weapon. "I am acting under duress," the chief said drily. "Nice to have somebody looking out for your interests."

Joe gawked. Margaret meant business. But any man aboard could just as easily have blown her away first. Then, looking into Gorson's almost-smile, Joe knew that no matter what everybody knew, nobody was ever going to admit it. It was, he supposed, nice to be home. He gave Gorson Lilly's limp hand.

Gorson coughed. "Do I have to?"

Joe gave the chief a bleak look.

"Yeah," Gorson growled. "I suppose we got to—unless we want to be just like him." He hauled the unconscious weapons man aboard. He coughed again.

Lilly's face was still puffy from a Mexican boat hook. Now Theodore's brands would be superimposed.

The next thing Joe noticed was where they were. The *Alice* was drifting gently in the shallows of Lake Ascania—in plain sight of Nicaea. From the summer palace less than half a mile away a boatful of grimfaced men already rowed rapidly *Alice*ward, urged on by a priest in the bows who waved a smoking censer and chanted what was probably an exorcism.

"Jesus Homoousios Christ!" Joe yelled. "We're land-locked and Lilly just did unto others. Let's split!"

He had hoped they would still be set up—perhaps have figured out by now how Dr. Greybull's version of the time machine worked. Instead, there was a grinding of motors as the roller reefing gear took in the main and jib. The hand-set mizzen turned the ketch slowly upwind, pointing away from the boatful of palace guards but there was not enough wind to move. The new boys struggled to take the mizzen in from the reset stump of mast while Rose fiddled with switches and finally the battery powered screw was moving the *Alice* southeast a foot a minute faster than the palace guard could row. Joe suspected if the priest chanting in the bows would direct his voice astern it just might make the difference.

"So what's new?" he asked when he had descended the cabin slide and found Cook and Dr. Greybull struggling with the apparatus while Freedy fiddled with his transistorized fathometer. Freedy coughed noisily and looked for a place to spit.

Abruptly the radioman spun and stuck his head out of the slide. "Full astern!" he yelled. Before Rose could react Joe felt the ketch sliding smoothly into mud. The screw whined loudly in the instant before the engineman reversed. Then blades cut into the mud bottom and the screw would not turn either way.

Joe sprang back into the cockpit and studied oarsmen limned in late afternoon sun. They still rowed but now that they knew the *Alice* was firmly aground the palace guard was having second thoughts about attacking powerful magicians with naught but swords and spears. So too, apparently, was the priest.

Then Joe saw what had changed their mind. Standing near naked on the stern counter their newly recuited Indian— Baakot?—was dancing and chanting his own magic. Where the priest had waved a censer, the Indian's teeth grasped one of Rose's cigars. Puffing to the four winds, he directed a gesture very like the unfortunate Athanasius' at the gaping palace guard. Baakot puffed vigorously. It was the first time these third century men had ever seen tobacco. The Indian was blowing enough smoke to elect a president. He also seemed the only man aboard who was not coughing.

Joe scampered below again. "Fellows" he said, "I don't like to breathe down your neck but—"

"Try pumping now." Dr. Graybull ignored Joe. Cook humped over the handy billy and struggled to create a vacuum inside an inverted plastic bucket. The sides of the bucket began to distort inward, delineating the framework someone had cobbled up to prevent this.

Freedy came down the ladder stiffly and one-handed, trying to hold broken glasses together with the other. He began flipping ranges and running scales on the fathometer.

Nothing happened.

Joe looked topside again. The priest had finally pumped up his courage and the palace guard was rowing very slowly toward the *Alice*. Joe guessed he had another minute. Jesus!

He had not intended to wreck the world. Now—if Theodore was right—there was nothing to go back to.

Which simplified one thing. If there was no future then Joe need have no qualms about screwing up the past. "Lilly!" he bawled, then remembered that particular albatross was no longer around his neck. He wished most devoutly that he had killed Lilly before the weapons man could have done all his deviltry.

"Sir!" It was Gorson. "I been poking through his stuff."

Joe studied the chief. "Can you make them go away? Don't kill the poor bastards unless you have to."

Gorson stooped and selected a weapon. He coughed and hacked for a moment and then controlled himself. There was a pop-whoosh as he fired a rocket. When a cubic meter of lake erupted noisily just forward of the barge several rowers caught crabs as men ahead and behind backed oars.

"Goo'!" Baakot observed. "Goo', good!"

"Our feathered friend has learned one word of English," Gorson explained.

"And now," Joe growled, "How do we get out of this mud?"

"Without tides?" Gorson asked mournfully. "You might ask those clowns over there to take a line ashore so we can kedge off."

Joe doubted if the palace guard would prove that cooperative. "Dr. Greybull," he called, "Have you any idea what's wrong?"

"Of course I do. That damned Indian called a preemptive strike against measles and smallpox. He poisoned us with his sniffles or his turtle stew or whatever."

"I mean with the time machine," Joe protested.

"We discharged the batteries with the last few jumps," Greybull explained. "Give us a few sunny days and they'll come up again."

Joe sighed. This was not going to be a fun trip. How long could they outmaneuver the emperor's forces on a lake ten miles long and three wide?

Chapter 18

Joe was about to ask Rose if there was no other way to charge batteries when he heard the preliminary wheeze, then the steady popping of a small engine. Joe compared the size of the generator and the size of the batteries and knew there would be no relief for many hours. There was a sudden gust. Clouds were piling up in the southeast.

The sun went down and in the day's last light Joe noted that the city side of the lakeshore was filled with gawkers out to watch the emperor's forces kill the magicians. He glanced up in the rigging and Margaret White still sat with an automatic weapon in her lap. "For Christ's sake, come on down!" Joe called. "Somebody'll practice archery on you. What're you doing up there?"

Margaret descended stiffly, looking very small and helpless in Joe's oversized dungarees. "Are you all right?" she asked.

"Shouldn't I ask you that once in a while?"

She gave him an unfathomable look. "I'm sleepy," she finally said.

"Trouble with the men? "

"The cook came on like an Old Testament prophet," Margaret said. "Nobody's looked at me since."

"How is Cook?"

"Coughing. He came down with it first. Dr. Greybull thinks it was something in that turtle he handled and cooked. Do you mind if I go sleep in your cabin?"

"After that valiant vigil aloft it would seem the least I can do. What were you doing up there?"

"The chief said you'd ordered him not to come back for you."

"And you didn't believe him?"

"You didn't tell me."

"You're—" Joe sighed. Margaret sometimes tended to forget chain-of-command. But she had always covered for him. The *Alice's* people would, he supposed, have witnessed her vigil with some amusement. Then he realized that Gorson's amusement was tinged with envy. "Go below and rest," Joe said. He devoted himself to trying to figure how they were going to get off a mudbank before everyone in Nicaea came out to scrag the magicians.

The *Alice* had once drawn six feet. A couple of inches more, he supposed, in fresh water. But what difference did it make? There was no physical way off this mudflat before the emperor and his irate bishops could— But how had they connected up the assassination with the appearance of a seagoing ship in their private lake?

Joe concluded that it did not require any deductive facility. One unexplained event plus another add up to sorcery. Even if Bishop Theodore's friend had not been spreading the word. Was the other man also from the modern era? Speaking Russian would help explain why Joe couldn't follow their Greek.

So what? Joe knew with a visceral conviction that it was all over now. No time stream could remain unchanged after Lilly passed through it.

"Joe?" It was Gorson. "Want me to hand out weapons?"

Joe nodded. It was turning dark but fires blazed along the

shore in front of the palace. There was the boom of a drum and the blat of a regimental *tuba*. "What've we got?"

"Pistolilly still had a couple of those heatseeking bazooka repeaters stashed in the chain locker. Cook's learned to hit the narrow end of a barn."

"What about the rest of us?" Joe asked. "We may have to repel boarders soon."

"M-16s." Gorson squinted shoreward where men were preparing by firelight to launch another barge. He looked a question at Joe.

"Worth a try," Joe said.

Gorson aimed the heatseeker at the largest of the fires along the beach. The rocket left a fiery zigzag trail and then the fire on the beach erupted into a shower of sparks. "Might give us another half hour," Gorson said as men on shore scattered. The breeze was steadying now that the sun was welldown and the land-sea flow shifted direction. Joe studied it.

The wind was from ahead—in the right direction to take the *Alice* off the mudflats but even if they could guy sails around the wind would not be enough. The shore ahead was two or three miles around from the palace and a mile airline, its final hundred yards an indistinct mass of reeds and cattails. Joe was staring bleakly into gathering darkness when a fire blazed. Thunderheads obscured the sky above the fire.

"Wonder why they'd try from that angle?" Gorson growled.

"I'm afraid I know," Joe said. The fire was small but intense. It was moving. Already it had drifted past the cattails into open water. It was less than half a mile from the *Alice*, and closing rapidly. The wind was pushing the fireship straight toward them.

Cook came on deck. "What's that?"

"Pitch, olive oil, turpentine, and possibly a little sulfur," Joe said. "The emperor's engineers will have timed it for the container to burn through about the time it's closest to us. The burning mass will float and spread just like gasoline."

"Time's a wastin'!" Cook fired.

The joyous shoreside shout aborted as they realized Cook had blown up the fireship prematurely. As a wall of fire moved down on the *Alice* Joe wondered if they might not better have waited and hoped it would drift by. Gorson and Cook were both coughing again. Joe caught a whiff of the heavy sulfurous smoke and then he was coughing too. "All hands!" he yelled. "Man the buckets! Anything to wet us down!"

Rose had anticipated him with handy billys. Two of the new boys humped over the pumps while the engineman hosed foetid, swampy water over the ketch's topsides. The stench of burning pitch and sulfur was rapidly becoming unendurable for men already coughing from whatever bug the Indian had brought. Through all the confusion came the steady popping of the tiny generator that was topping up the batteries and would be ready to get them out of here only a day or two late. "Pump, you evil magicians!" Joe yelled. "If they don't burn us here they will ashore!"

The evening breeze brought a hundred foot wide sheet of flame toward the *Alice*. Joe wondered how long it would burn. Wouldn't reach the ketch, he prayed, or else the emperor's engineers would have triggered it to fire before Cook's rocketry. But the smoky yellow-blue flicker was so close he had to shield his face from the heat. He snatched a bucket and scooped water over himself. He wet down the coughing, retching boys who manned the pumps, sloshed Gorson and the others who struggled to save the *Alice*. And still the fire came.

But it was starting to burn out. As the flame front cooled the smoke and sulfur stink grew. Eyes streaming, he sloshed another bucket over himself and hastened to wet down the others. There was a sudden agonized sneeze and the generator engine quit.

Joe struggled with yet another bucket of water and then abruptly he was reeling, throat burning as sulfur dioxide contacted mucus and became sulfurous acid. He sat dizzy on the edge of the cockpit.

There was a final guttering whump and the fire went out. Men sprawled on the *Alice's* deck coughing and hacking. Joe forced himself to his feet. What was he doing crapping out when these others were already sick from some unknown virus? Air in the cockpit was unbreathable. Standing, it was a little better. "Hold your breath and hang on," he yelled. "It's blowing away."

Margaret was handing out pads of dampened gauze. Joe accepted one and got a breath of almost clean air. "What next?" she asked.

Joe searched in the darkness and found the binoculars. The 7x50 night glasses gave him an indistinct view of the shore ahead but he saw no more preparations. Perhaps they would wait till dawn for their next attempt. Or did they think they had succeeded? "Quiet," he cautioned. Behind, toward the palace the shore was also dark. Joe supposed they had deduced that fires drew the magicians' lightning.

What was all this doing to the time stream?

Rose was securing hose and handy billys. "You all right?" Joe asked.

"I'm sixteen hundred years from home," the engineman growled. "I'm fifty years old, and I'm sick."

"Any idea what happened to the generator?"

"Don't ask."

"I suppose I'll have to."

"It's wired with a negative bias," Rose explained. "Shuts off automatically when the batteries are charged."

"Then we can get out of here!"

"Don't count on it. All that fire and smoke just cooked our solar collectors. Probably gave one final dying gasp and that's what shut it off."

Joe went below and broke the news to Dr. Greybull who still puttered ineffectually with his suitcaseful of malfunctioning electronics.

"What is our situation here?" the scientist asked.

"You know Dr. Lilly's talent for making friends," Joe said. Lilly lay pale and prostrate on the galley settee, breathing regularly and heavily. Joe glanced at him.

"Equal dilation in both pupils," Greybull said to Joe's unspoken question. "Considering his general indestructibility, we'll probably have to deal with Dr. Lilly again soon."

Joe sighed. He would gladly have killed the weapons man on several occasions. But what was the point of killing anybody now?

"So the collectors are dead and the batteries dying," Greybull summed up. "I don't know how we'll ever manage a jump all the way home but if I read you correctly, just about anything is better than here?"

There was a wheezing pop and then the generator was running again. And that was the end of any hope that those ashore might think they had put an end to the *Alice*. Rose came below, still breathing unsteadily through a pad of wet gauze.

"Do we have enough fuel or any hope that little cornpopper will ever top up the batteries?" Joe asked.

"If you turn everything else off and I can manage to keep it running for a couple of days," Rose said.

"Goo'—good!" Baakot was immensely cheerful for a man wrenched from home without explanation. Or perhaps Kraus had gotten through to the Indian.

"I doubt if they'll give us a couple of days," Joe said.

"Somehow I had the same feeling," Rose said. Turning to Dr. Greybull he asked, "Have you ever worked it out in kilowatts or joules or whatever?"

"I beg your pardon?"

"How much power do we need for a jump? If it's just some kind of a triggering voltage then maybe I can hook all the batteries up in series instead of parallel. Wouldn't give you any real power but you ought to get a second or two of surge before they quit."

Dr. Greybull was uncertain. "I suppose we lose nothing by trying," he said.

And a great deal by not trying, Joe thought.

Rose began lifting the cabin floorboards to expose the ranks of lead-acid cells that powered the *Alice*. "You realize," he said offhandedly, "that I'm cannibalizing cable to make all these connections. Doubtful if I'll ever have enough to hook them back up the right way.''

"We know," Joe said. "Who do you want to help you?"

"Gorson and Hennis."

Behind them on the settee Lilly moaned. Joe looked at him but the weapons man was still unconscious. Joe went on deck. Now that they didn't need the water it was starting to rain.

Chapter 19

Joe studied the sky. Within minutes this gentle rain was going to become a cloudburst. Was there the slightest chance of the lake's rising enough to float the *Alice*? Gorson came on deck and handed Joe his oilskins. "No point in you coming down with it too," the chief growled.

"We've got to get out of here." Joe was talking to himself.

"We'll end up farther in the past. Christians are bad enough," the chief added. "You want to go back and fight real Romans again?"

Joe did not. But Gorson had reminded him of something. "Our old machine used power to move back and this one needs power to move us forward in time. Do you see what's coming?"

Gorson looked at the clouds and shook his head. "At sea, maybe. We're in a lake bottom with high ground and buildings all around. No lightning's ever going to strike us."

"Gorson, where are those cohabitating cable cutters?" It was Rose.

Joe turned to the engineman. "See the weather building?"

"Fat lot of good it'll do us in this hole."

"I wonder if Benjamin Franklin felt that way."

"Son of a bitch!" Gorson remarked. "And Pistolilly brought some too!"

"Some what?" Rose demanded.

"Target kites for gunnery practice."

"But we haven't got any wire."

"Neither did Franklin," Joe said.

Rose shrugged. "Worth a try, I guess." The engineman seemed unconvinced.

The next time Joe stuck his head down the galley slide Gorson, Cook, and Rose were putting together a six foot plastic-and-aluminum-tubing kite with a stylized airplane stenciled on its lower surface. Abruptly the pop-popping of the generator engine ceased.

"Thank you, Jesus," Gorson snarled. Rose went to change the fuel filter again. By the time he had it running Gorson and Cook had launched the kite successfully—after two dives into the shallow water around the *Alice*—and were paying out string. Joe studied the rising wind and hoped it would work.

Dr. Greybull hunched over his malfunctioning suitcase, watching Freedy who stood poised at the fathometer, and Hennis who manned the makeshift handy-billy vacuum pump. All it required was for everyone to get to work at the proper instant and coordinate their efforts with a stroke of lightning.

Dr. Greybull nodded at Hennis. The gangling black started pumping slowly. The plastic bucket began deforming inward around its internal framework. Freedy struggled to hold his glasses together while turning on the fathometer. Joe struggled to betray no emotion.

"You don't seem particularly optimistic," Dr. Greybull observed.

Joe tried to smile and could not. He knew that a time jump would not really improve anything. No matter where or when they went they would take themselves and Lilly's tempollution with them. The door to his cabin opened and Margaret White stepped out. She seemed tired but she was clean, her blonde hair combed, and she bore no visible defects.

"Nice to see that you still react to some things," Dr. Greybull added with a quiet smile. "Gad, if I were only sixty again!"

Joe went back on deck to see how the kite was doing. At that instant it did. Thunder deafened him. Lightning blinded him. He sensed the familiar flicker-shimmer and when he collected his blasted wits the *Alice* was no longer in the mud. The ketch was rolling violently. It was still dark and the wind was blowing harder now. Something wraithlike moved at him in the darkness and Joe ducked in panic in the instant before he saw it was the carbonized memory of a kite string whipping off alee. They were in the middle of a storm but at least the *Alice* was moving. They were at sea.

"You know," Gorson shouted, "Catching lightning gets old after a while." The chief chivvied a work party on deck and they began rigging life lines.

"Goo'!"

Joe jumped again. The Indian was grinning in wholehearted approval. He began talking rapidly in yaqui. Joe shook his head. The Indian was insistent. "Kraus!" Joe finally called, "See if you can find out what he wants." Joe went below to see what bad news Freedy would give him with the fathometer. From the ground swell Joe suspected they were, at very least, on a continental shelf and possibly in even more shallow water.

"Sixteen fathoms," the radioman said. "Radar shows land about 60 miles east. Looks like an island behind us too."

"Goo', good!" Baakot was pointing east, practically dancing with excitement.

"Go ahead," Joe said. "One direction's as good as another." Then he halted. "Nothing on the radio, I suppose?"

Freedy shook his head and grabbed at his falling glasses. "Guess we're still stuck somewhere in the past," he said.

Rose stuck his head up out of the opened cabin sole. "Might as well set up a little wind generator," he said. "Gasoline's about shot and all this bouncing around stirs up crud faster'n I can change filters anyhow."

"Do we have to?" Kraus asked.

"Only if you want hot meals," Cook said.

"Are we reasonably secure for a few hours?" Joe asked.

"Guess so." Gorson coughed again.

"Who needs sleep the worst?"

"Reckon you do," Cook said.

Behind them on the settee the unconscious Lilly groaned.

Joe surveyed his cabin door. Margaret was up. He guessed it was his turn to use the bunk.

Gorson was shaking him.

"Yeah?"

"Land in sight."

"I can hardly wait," Joe said. But he got up and splashed his face clean at the salt water tap.

When he went on deck the Indian was even more excited. "Goo'," Baakot assured him.

"He knows where we are," Kraus said.

"Does he know when?"

Kraus struggled to interpret this, and ran into his usual snags over the Amerind concept of time. Finally he threw up his hands. "Good harbor and good water," he says. "Good fish an' lots food."

It was the best news Joe had received in some time. Then he reflected on the darker side of it. In dealing with primitives Joe had longsince discovered that *gift* is an unfortunate word for what usually turns into organized extortion. The Indians would load him down with fish and fruit and other perishables he didn't really need. What was he to give them in return?

Baakot would assume their supply of floating-handled steel knives to be unlimited. There would be the usual misunderstandings and hard feelings. And history would blame it all on the white man. He studied Kraus, wondering if there was any way to get some warning across to the other Indian. It was going to turn into another fight—another disaster. Joe knew it!

What he ought to do, Joe thought—best for all concerned—would be to put Baakot adrift near shore in a life raft and bug out before they killed somebody else. Joe suggested this to Kraus and was rewarded by a look of respect and perhaps affection.

Kraus tried to explain it to Baakot. Finally he threw up his hand and turned to Joe. "He say you come shore talk to his mother."

Joe could not understand it. Yaquis had fought the Spaniards to a standstill—until the wave of conquest parted and flowed around their valley. Yaquis, Kraus agreed, had always fought to repel strangers from their land. If they had actually managed to get Baakot back to his own time this was too early for them to have learned that all whites were not Spaniards, or that someday gringos would sell them weapons. But . . . they had to put in somewhere and refit. The *Alice* still needed a new mizzen mast. With misgivings, Joe agreed to take the Indian home.

As Baakot had predicted, there was a small harbor. On shore dugouts were drawn up high enough to indicate a respectable tide. From the way their owners jumped up and down, screaming threats and brandishing bows Joe concluded that these people had enjoyed previous contacts with European culture.

The *Alice* came up into the wind a mile offshore.

"Four," Freedy called, and switched off the fathometer.

"Drop it?" Gorson asked. Two of the larger dugouts had pushed off and were paddling toward them.

"Not yet," Joe said. "Heave to and we'll see if our friend is talking through his feathers. "Meanwhile—by the way, is Lilly still out of action?"

Gorson nodded.

"I guess you can trust the others with weapons," Joe decided. "But let's see if we can't, just this once in our drab and wretched lives, make a peaceable contact.''

All hands crowded the rail. As the dugouts came closer Joe saw they were the typical *canoas* still in use along the Pacific coast of both Americas. There was, he realized, no art quite so hidebound in tradition and conservatism as shipbuilding.

The men dressed much as did Baakot, in loincloth and with an occasional feather. Their paddles were huge, spear-shaped, ornately carved and not, Joe suspected, particularly efficient. In the bow of each *canoa* a man stood brandishing a round targetlike shield and a *maqualatl*, which flintstudded club is stone age man's precursor to the sword.

''*Achaim!*'' Baakot had climbed the rigging and was in plain view above the rest of the *Alice's* people. He began a harangue and abruptly the threats were ended.

From the Indian's willingness to join them without looking back Joe had suspected that he would turn out to be some kind of pariah in the community but once again Joe discovered that he was wrong. Unless he was totally misreading the signals Baakot was a man of considerable substance. The warriors in the *canoas* gave him the respectful attention due to an elder orator.

''Is he the chief?'' Joe asked Kraus.

The boy shook his head. ''They got no chief,'' he explained. ''Old wise woman.'' He shook his head. ''Sea woman?''

''You've never heard of this before?''

Kraus had not.

Joe supposed he would find out soon enough. Baakot finished his speechmaking and there was an awed silence in the *canoas*. After a moment two men transferred from one to the other, which was now within an inch of swamping. Baakot turned to Joe. ''Goo','' he explained.

Joe supposed the only way to find out whether it was good or not was to accept the Indian's insistence that he accompany them ashore. He turned to Kraus. ''I'll need an interpreter. You want to go?''

Kraus was eager to dig into his roots.

''You think it's a good idea?'' Gorson muttered.

"I don't know what else to do," Joe said.

"Shove that Indian over the side and light a shuck out of here," Cook suggested. "He's home. What more's he want?"

"Beats me," Joe said. "But have you ever seen a guy so friendly for so little reason?"

Cook had not.

"You may as well drop the hook till I come back. But if anything happens my former instructions stand."

Gorson raised his eyebrows. "No rescue? You better clue in your yeoperson. Besides, I wouldn't feel right without wasting a few rounds of Pistolilly's ammo."

"No more killing. Give me six hours." Turning to Kraus he asked, "Can you find some polite way of letting those folks in the *canoas* know my people want me back before noon?"

While Kraus was struggling to explain Gorson tossed a flaming molotov cocktail astern, well away from the *canoas* and used one of Lilly's heatseekers to blow it up along with a cubic meter of ocean.

The Indians were neither awed nor frightened. They were nodding and enthusiastic in their approval. "Shall we go?" The *Alice's* people lined the rail watching their captain being paddled a mile back to the shore. Joe thought he saw Margaret.

To Joe it seemed a miracle that they ever reached the beach but, although the *canoa* was plunging through breakers with less than an inch of freeboard, the Indians got him ashore with only his feet wet.

Kraus was looking about the inlet in a state of subdued awe. "I been here," he finally whispered.

"Yeah?"

"Bacochibampo. That beach—that little island." Kraus straightened and sniffed the pristine air.

"Where's Bacochibampo?"

"Two—three kilometers from Guaymas. My folks went home winters when I was kid."

A suspicion began growing in Joe. "Baakot—Bacochi?"

"Bacochibampo is snake water." Then Kraus's mouth opened. "Or the harbor belongs man call' snake!"

"We seem to have stumbled onto another historical character," Joe said. "What was he famous for?"

"I don' know," Kraus protested. "I never knew he—"

Baakot was leading them through the random scatter of wattle and daub, thatch roofed huts that made up the village. A hundred men, women, and children studied them, discussed them, and mimicked the white man's strange toes-out gait with a total lack of stoicism. The walls of the houses were high enough for privacy but lacked an ell of closing with the eaves. In this Turkish bath climate it was the only practical style of architecture.

Joe supposed he was being conducted to some council of the village elders. Since the largest house was only meters away it was pointless to ask. Baakot turned and bestowed his fullwattage smile on Joe and Kraus. "Goo'!" he said, and pushed them through the low doorway of the village big house.

Joe stooped and scooted through. He sensed Kraus beside him but after brilliant sunlight on water and sand he was blind. He closed his eyes and waited. When vision returned he saw an old woman seated on a blanket across the single ovalshaped room. She was alone. She was looking at them with a singular intensity.

"Looks like we've met the wise woman," Joe muttered. "Give her your best shot."

"Dios em chiokwe, maalayo' owe," Kraus began.

Abruptly the old woman's expression changed. She seemed—disappointed. They stared at each other for a silent moment. Joe shrugged. "Sorry," he muttered. "Were you expecting somebody else?"

"No fablais qualcuna lingua christiana?" the old woman asked.

Joe felt a sudden frisson at the archaic phrasing. Surely sixteenth century Spanish did not sound like this. But . . . old speech patterns persisted for centuries in out of the way places. His eyes were accustoming to the darkness and he saw this was no Indian woman. "¿Art thou captive?" he asked. "¿Hast been here long?"

The old woman sighed. "A long life," she said. "But not a bad one. I have my health and my grandchildren. And whence come you sirs?"

Chapter 20

Joe cursed himself for not having prefabricated something believable. How was he going to explain time travel? The old woman was waiting. "We—uh—came out of the sea," he said lamely.

The wise woman gave a sad smile. "I also came out of the sea. Fishermen from this village rescued me." She regarded her hands folded in her lap. "And then one married me. Did you lose many people when your ship sank?"

"We didn't sink. We're anchored half a league offshore."

"Ah? Give me your hand."

Joe helped the old woman to her feet. She was small and stoopshouldered but bore herself with that assurance that stems from the memory of unchallenged beauty. There was a milky hint of cataract in her dark eyes. "Stick here somewhere," she murmured. Kraus found it and put it in her hand. The old woman hobbled to the door of the hut and emitted a reedy whistle.

Two young men appeared and made a chair-seat with their arms. They bore the old woman shoreward while Joe and

Kraus followed bemused by the reverence with which the villagers greeted their wise woman. Joe saw that it was not just superstitious fear. No one seemed afraid of her.

He was still wondering what cultural edge a shipwrecked woman could have possessed that would make her useful among Spaniard-hating Indians when the young men got their wise woman situated amidships in a *canoa* with Kraus in front and Joe behind.

Boys and girls well into puberty played naked about the village but matrons wore all-enveloping *tilmatli* that hung below their knees and did not require separate skirts. The old woman's dress was no different. Her white hair was braided and coiled high in a *molote* like most adult men and women. She settled into the dugout and rode with unconcerned serenity through crashing surf.

Gorson and Cook bent over the rail to lift her aboard. Gorson gave the old woman an odd look and glanced sharply at Cook.

"Ain't no Injun," Cook muttered.

"Where'd you find her?" Gorson asked.

"Ashore. She seems to run the place."

Gorson studied Joe. "Don't you know her?"

It was Joe's turn to stare.

Gorson was shaking his head. "Course not," he growled. "You're still looking for a memory."

Margaret was at the bottom of the cabin slide, helping the old woman as the two young Indians handed her down. Joe followed. The old woman blinked in the belowdecks darkness but she walked unerringly forward, through the galley, through the fo'c's'l, to the edge of the chain locker. She put her hand in and felt the coils of hot-stretch nylon used to extend the anchor chain. She stood very still for a moment, then turned slowly. "Joe?" she asked. "You do not know me?"

"Oh my God!" He did not know if the wail was for himself or for the old woman. Joe and this crone had been young together. For her memory he had severed himself from all human connection, hunting a dream—and now he had found it. "Raquel!" From the corner of his vision he saw Gorson and Cook. He saw Freedy. All hands stared at Joe and his old girl friend.

Including Margaret.

"Joe?" The old woman was uncertain. "All the years I told the fishermen to look for strange men and a ship from another time. I know this is the ship. But are you Joe?"

From behind the galley table came a sudden moan from the still-unconscious Lilly.

"Yes, I'm Joe. I'm old now too."

The old woman laughed. "How long has it been for you?"

"Almost fifteen years."

"For me it has been closer to sixty."

Joe wanted to shriek and howl. He wanted to take hammer to their statues and smear dung on the deities who had permitted this. Choking with rage, he directed his middle finger skyward. "You'll pay your debt to me," he promised.

Margaret stood silent beside the old woman, helping her to stand against the slight movement at anchor in the roadstead.

"But surely there's a way—" Dr. Greybull began. "I read the reports. I know what she must—" Abruptly the scientist broke off.

"Go back sixty years and pick her up young? Go ahead until I'm her age? Wipe out a life that was not shared and create a new simulacrum?" When they stared he realized he had been speaking in the same 10th century Spanish that he and Raquel had once shared.

From behind the galley table Lilly emitted a prolonged sigh. Joe looked as the weapons man stirred and stretched. He waited a moment but Lilly did not regain consciousness.

"What of you?" Raquel asked. "Do your children prosper?"

Joe spread his hands.

Raquel came close and strained to see through cloudy eyes. Joe bent and put his arms around her. "You grow older," she said. "How many sons have you?"

"I kept looking for you."

Raquel pushed him away. "Alone?" she asked with grow-

ing horror. "Squander your life for the memory of a stranger
you knew perhaps a month?" She shook her head. "You saw
my grandsons. I have others. My life has not been wasted
here. Had I fallen in with my own Christian kind—" She
shrugged. "Would I have ended up as some conquistador's
concubine? Would the years have pushed me from bedroom
to kitchen?" She struggled to see through cataracts. "My
poor Joe. I thought better of you."

"Grandsons?" Then Joe knew they must be the young
men who had carried her down to the dugout. "You're
right," he said. "My life is wasted. My world is wasted.
Neither was much loss."

Raquel squinted and tried to see him. "Was I so different?" she asked. "We were young. It would have been nice.
But it didn't happen. I've had a good life. There is time for
you."

"*¿Con quién?*" he asked. "With whom? Some other
middleaged failure?"

The wise woman from the sea smiled and for the first time
Joe saw Raquel amid the ruins. "Fifty years ago I would have
killed any woman who looked at you like this heartsick child
who helps me to stand."

She did not understand 10th century Spanish but Margaret
sensed the charge of emotion. To Joe it was abruptly apparent
that if all the evil in the universe had conspired, no infinitude
of devils could ever have achieved the catastrophe he had
created from the raw material of a single, rather ordinary life.

All he had ever asked was to be left alone. The walls he had
built around himself had done what no malevolent god could
have. He had not just spoiled his own life. In his frantic
struggle to avoid more pain he had managed to fuck up every
life line that crossed his. Even Lilly's!

Joe's life held few secrets. Margaret had managed his
affairs and concealed his deficiencies. She would have come
across unclassified bits and snippets of the *Alice's* log. She
would have pumped Gorson and Cook, Freedy—anyone
who remembered the old days. Margaret White knew who
this whitehaired old woman had to be. "Sorry," she said.

Joe nodded. "Aren't we all!"

Kraus stuck his head down the cabin slide. "Sir," he said, "They gettin' jumpy out here. Maybe you bring the old lady topside where they see she's all right?" He added a swift paraphrase in Yaqui and Raquel nodded. She moved back through the *Alice's* fo'c's'l, through the galley, touching bunks and bulkheads, saying farewell to the unfinished business of youth. Grandsons reached down to help her up the cabin slide.

Lilly groaned again. He had changed position but remained unconscious. Joe gave Greybull a harried look. "No change," the older man said. "I smeared burn ointment and bandaged his hands. Coma could drag on for weeks."

On deck Cook was conducting a lively barter with *canoas* that surrounded the *Alice* in alarming numbers. If the Indians were to revert to their normal attitude toward strangers there would be a bit of a problem. Cook, though, limited his preocupation to the number of fresh oysters he could secure for a jelly bean.

Raquel had retreated to her favorite refuge up in the bows. She sat leaning against the samson post, flanked by Margaret and young Kraus, who was the only interpreter apart from Joe. Her grandsons squatted at a respectable distance passing one of Rose's cigars back and forth as they struggled to keep it lit. Joe considered joining the women but he sensed that his presence was not desired.

"Doesn't seem to be much straight timber available," Rose said as he studied tortured clumps of mezquite and chaparral just up from the high tide mark.

Joe suspected his engineman wanted conversation more than he wanted a new mizzen mast. "I'll survive," Joe said. "People always do."

"That's the hell of it."

"Ever marry?" Joe asked.

"How do you suppose I learned about hell?"

"There must be other ways."

"Looks like you found your own."

"Why me? What did I do?"

Rose gave him a fishy look and took longer than necessary to relight his stub of cigar. "You the first man ever lost a girl?" he asked. "Women change their minds. Just when I thought I could count on one—twenty three years and then she up and died on me. No damned consideration at all!"

Joe had been too immersed in his own misery to inform himself. "Will you marry again?"

"First chance I get."

Joe gave his engineman a bleak look.

"People don't want to couldn't've been very happy the first time around," Rose said. "I was. I'll find somebody else who was too. We'll patch the pieces together and enjoy what's left. You're young enough to moon about a romantic past that never was. Man my age looks to the future."

Joe felt as if someone had dumped a bucket of ice water on him. "Knew I was a fool," he muttered. "Just didn't know I was stupid." He reminded himself that Lilly had precluded any normal lifeline for those aboard the *Alice*. What kind of existence awaited them? Whatever, he would have to emerge from the cocoon of his private misery and take care of his people. Margaret White was one of them.

Trading had tapered off and most of the village *canoas* had withdrawn. Only the one that had brought Raquel out to the *Alice* still drifted off a painter astern. The paddlers and Raquel's grandsons had satisfied their curiosity and now lounged amidships listening to Baakot who, Joe suspected from his gestures, was dramatizing their escape from the Nicaean palace guard.

Up in the bow Raquel and Margaret were still in deep converse. Carving up Joe, he supposed. He tried not to be apathetic. A man should take an interest in his life.

Endless what-ifs raced through his mind. If he had killed Lilly? If he'd acted sooner or more decisively on any of a thousand turning points in the time stream . . . if he'd just come home quietly from that first expedition and never said anything . . .

If he'd forgotten it and settled down and lived his life like like normal people it would have made no difference at all for

Raquel except that he would not be here now reopening old wounds. Should have given Commander Cutlott some other cock-and-bull story. The *Alice's* people would have been willing enough to pretend it never happened. All they had ever gotten out of time travel was misery and blighted careers. He stood braced against the jury rigged mizzen glaring astern at the *canoa* which bobbed inoffensively at the end of its painter.

If only the damned machine were controllable perhaps he could really go back and change things. But it worked by some whim of its own. Greybull was right. The thing did react with the operator. Like djinn or leprechaun, the time machine granted wishes. Joe's prayers had been answered. In the future he would be more careful what he prayed for. Damned flicker-shimmering machine! Abruptly he realized he was not imagining it. The *Alice* was making another time jump. Tension eased on the painter to the *canoa*. It began wriggling into curves and coils. The end of the rope was cut off sharp and the *canoa* was gone.

Good God, he had Raquel and half a dozen Indians aboard!

Chapter 21

Joe tore his hair and gnashed his teeth as he charged down the cabin slide into the galley. "Is it asking too much to let me know?" he snarled. "I'm still supposed to be the captain!" Then he saw who had done it.

Looking like warmed over death, Lilly was on his feet again, fumbling with Dr. Greybull's suitcaseful of capricious electronics. Somehow the weapons man had managed to pump on a handy billy while fiddling with fathometer range switches and various adjustments inside the suitcase. And all this with bandaged hands! There was no triumphant grin on the security expert's battered face this time. "Don't worry, sir, we'll make it yet." Lilly's voice was hoarse with strain and pain.

Should have killed him while I could. But as Joe surveyed this wreck he knew he was sucking wind. Lilly didn't need killing. He needed a bed in a maximum security ward. Gorson came below. He looked at Joe.

"Any ideas?" Joe asked.

The chief shrugged. "Stretch out," he told Lilly. "You still need to rest."

Lilly studied him blearily and, to Joe's surprise, lay down.

"Got any red-and-yellows in your stash?" the chief asked.

Joe went to his cabin and rummaged through the *Alice's* limited medical supplies for dalmane. Gorson disappeared and returned with a fifth of Old Crow. Lilly swallowed the capsules without comment and washed them down with whiskey. Within minutes he was snoring again.

"And now," Gorson growled, "What did he get us into?"

Freedy was already spinning dials on the radio. "Must still be in the past," he said, then abruptly halted to fine-tune something. The faint voice was in English. "—all the locals have packed up. Not enough clean ground to plant anything. How're you?"

The reply was louder. "Raiders around here so we sell protection. We get on pretty good with the farmers. What's that?"

Unwittingly, Joe's clenched fist had squeezed the transmit button and they had heard the click.

"My antenna's miles away and booby trapped," the first voice said, "but there's no sense sending an invitation. Over and out."

"Who the hell is it?" the louder voice demanded.

"U.S. Navy ship *Alice,*" Joe replied. "Anything we can do to help?"

"You can fuck off. Ain't been no navy since eighty nine."

"What's the date now?" Joe asked.

"Where you been? Moon base?"

What was the point of lying? Nobody was going to believe anything he said. "We've been time traveling," Joe said. "What year is this?"

"Nineteen ninety four I think. What difference's it make?"

Not much, Joe guessed. "Is there anything left? Any government at all?"

"You're talking to it. If you really are navy good luck to you. You'll never get a ship through the mountains no matter how you triangulate on this signal."

"Could you tell us where *we* are?"

"You're either 225° southwest or 45° northeast. Since the latter would put you in Lake Tahoe I'd guess you're somewhere off Southern California. On a clear day you can see Catalina but don't look for Los Angeles."

Margaret and Raquel's grandsons had helped the old lady below. "You still cannot make it work right?" Raquel asked.

"Good luck and hang onto your batteries," the radio voice said. "If you guys really are time travelers maybe you could go back and burn the son of a bitch that started this war. Over and out."

"Wait a minute!" Joe protested. "Did anybody win? Was it the Russians?"

"Who the hell are they? Look, we got some trouble outside the stockade. I gotta shut down now." The hiss of carrier wave died as the transmitter went off the air.

Those not on duty had crowded into the galley and caught most of it. Joe surveyed them bleakly.

"Too bad we didn't," Greybull said.

"Didn't what?"

"Burn the son of a bitch who started it." Dr. Greybull's voice was emotionless.

"All of us?" Joe asked.

Greybull shrugged. "It might be the only way."

"Why not just kill him?" Gorson pointed at the sleeping Lilly.

"What good would it do now?" Joe asked. "If we could have done it before he screwed everything up . . . if we could have sabotaged the expedition so he never got into the past . . ."

"We can," Greybull said.

"How?"

"Isn't our collective will stronger than his?"

Back on that sympathetic magic kick again, Joe supposed. "What do you propose?"

"Suicide."

"Be my guest," Gorson said. "I never did like civilians aboard."

"All of us."

"As an alternative we could all stay here," Joe said. "This era sounds like a real fun trip." He regarded the new boys and Raquel's grandsons—and Margaret. But when had life ever played fair?

"What do we gain by killin' ourselves?" Cook asked.

"Nothing unless we go back and put an end to this time tampering before it gets started."

"Can you get us back?" Joe asked.

"I can set up the machine," Dr. Greybull said tiredly. "Somebody who really cares had better throw the switch."

"Where exactly do you propose to do it?"

"Where it'll do the least amount of damage to the time stream," Greybull said. "Remember the accident in the harbor when we lost the mizzen mast?"

"What will happen?" Raquel asked.

"We did not live together," Joe said.

Raquel had not become the tribal wise woman for nothing. A life among Indians had taught her a way of backing obliquely into a subject instead of charging head on in the blunt European style. "So now we will die together?" She looked at her grandsons and sighed.

"I would not have had it this way," Joe said.

"I must tell them."

While Greybull, with Gorson and Cook's help struggled to set up the machine Joe noted that Baakot and his two sons made surprisingly little fuss when Raquel explained what was to happen. Then abruptly he wondered what *would* happen to them and Raquel. None had been aboard as the *Alice* was leaving harbor.

"Everyone ready?"

Joe had not expected it to happen so soon.

"Think good thoughts," Greybull said sardonically. "Who throws the switch?"

"I thought the batteries were shot," Joe said.

"Half of them are," Rose said, "but I've series-wired the rest and been charging them. If it really is just a triggering voltage . . . ." He left it dangling.

"*Morituri te salutamus,* Joe growled. He flipped the switch before he could change his mind. There was the familiar flicker-shimmer and sunlight ceased streaming through the portholes. He went on deck and strained his eyes into the darkness.

"Over there," Gorson said.

Joe squinted and got the binoculars back in focus. It had to be San Diego Bay. For the first time he began really to believe in Dr. Greybull's theory. Where the time machine put them *must* have something to do with the wish of the operator. But conscious or subconscious? In any crisis it seemed less reliable than prayer.

A heavily laden tuna clipper with some South American flag was wallowing up the channel. Behind it, closer to the city were the faint masthead lights of a sailing vessel under power. Joe swung the binoculars and saw with a sudden *frisson* that they had looped into another paradox. He stood in the cockpit and watched the ghostly silhouette of the *Alice* two miles off, heading toward itself.

Belatedly Joe discovered that he was still alive. With that last jump he had halfway expected that they might just wish themselves out of existence. He was tired, so mentally drained that anything seemed possible.

Now he saw that somehow they still had to destroy the original *Alice*. Or was this the original? Were they still a single ship? Would this ketch disappear if they sunk the other? But to blow up a navy ship in a busy channel was sure to leave time tracks that would screw things up as badly as they already were. He was still trying to guess how they might sink a ship inconspicuously when he saw Gorson hand up a rifle to Cook.

Cook put out the channel buoy light with his first shot. Gorson and Rose rigged a light on deck, using the batteries' last gasp to create a false buoy and lure the other *Alice* toward the invisible-at-high-tide rocks of the breakwater.

It would be impossible to damage her enough to kill everybody here in the harbor where people could swim or float ashore. "You'll have to use some of Lilly's rockets—"

he began. Then he saw the tug and tow coming up the channel, the tug's riding lights concealed behind the tuna clipper. The false buoy would draw the other *Alice* just far enough off course. This time she would not lose a mizzen mast. The tug would plow straight into the ketch and the huge screw would finish chopping up the pieces.

There was the faint shrilness of a siren. Then abruptly Joe knew it was a gas turbine.

"Oh shit!" Gorson moaned.

Joe was inclined to agree.

A launch was shrieking down the bay at forty knots, throwing great roostertails of spray. A searchlight came on and began sweeping the water around them.

Several possibilities raced through Joe's head. Buoy lights went out all the time and were routinely replaced next day. Had some sharpeyed observer in the Coast Guard tower known the bearing on the light and spotted the difference when it came on again? Or did somebody know the *Alice* would be duplicated at just this moment? There were more players in this game than Joe knew about. Where was Bishop Theodore right now? Where was Joe's sense of self-preservation?

"All hands below!" he yelled. "Greybull, flip that switch again. Quick!"

"What happened?"

"Somebody with good radar's coming out here to see what a ship without lights is doing impersonating a buoy."

"Oh dear!" Greybull murmured. "I hadn't expected that."

Gorson and Cook humped over the handy billy pumping a vacuum while Freedy ranged scales on the fathometer. The patrol boat was bellowing something over a loudspeaker about standing by for boarding when finally Joe felt the flicker-shimmer of a time jump. He was so relieved that he did not for a moment notice the glare coming through galley portholes. It was not daylight. The flicker was more like a fire.

The *Alice's* motion in a ground swell was unmistakable.

They were at sea over a shallow bottom. Then Joe knew what the fire was. Once more they were witnessing the explosion and burning of the rum runner that had been converted into a Mexican *guardacostas*. *My god!* he thought, *We're in a loop. Can we break out or will we just go round and round forever?*

But which turn of the loop was he in? Joe had seen this before—just as he had also sailed out of San Diego Bay and nearly gotten cut in two by a towing hawser before. But now there was only one *Alice*. He leaned over the gallery table to see if the drugged and battered weapons man still snored. Lilly was gone. Son of a bitch! After all those pills and booze? Not even the indestructible Lilly could manage that.

Then Joe knew where Lilly was—where he *had* to be.

There was still a chance to put things right. He had—what had been the nodal point here? Up on deck in the dark that night Joe had inspected the patent taffrail log. He had pulled in the spinner to clear it of seaweed and Lilly had . . .

Joe rushed for the cockpit, grabbing one of Cook's galley knives on the way. He sprinted astern for the log line. He was bending to cut it when Lilly erupted from the water and grabbed his arm. The knife splashed into the darkness.

This time Joe had been expecting something besides seaweed. Things had gone wrong because of his indecision. This time his decision was immediate. There was no point in killing everybody just to get rid of Lilly. As the weapons man swung his other arm out of the water and got a firmer grip Joe said farewell to all his problems. It was not a clean dive—not with Lilly hanging onto him—but Joe kicked himself a respectable distance away from the *Alice*. They floated side by side treading water as the ketch sailed away.

Chapter 22

"Not even going to yell?" Joe asked.

"It comes with the territory," Lilly said.

In the dying flicker of the gasoline fire Joe studied the ascetic planes and angles of the security man's face. Lilly did not seem overly troubled at the prospect of dying. "Perhaps the sharks will inspect this sector before we get tired of swimming," he said.

Joe had not thought about sharks. On balance he supposed they were preferable to treading water for several hours. "I hope you understand why I did it," he said.

"Never apologize," Lilly said. "And never explain." After a moment he added, "Of course I know. Things got a little out of hand. But when the Russians take over people like you'll remember me as part of the good old days."

Joe reminded himself that Lilly had been unconscious during their radio conversation with the grubby survivors of whatever had hit the fan. He had more trouble remembering that he was going to die. He had always thought death ought to be a solemn occasion. People made peace with their souls, with their gods. Joe discovered that he could put off even this decision.

He thought of Raquel, her sons and grandsons, and of Margaret. He knew he had made the right choice. The *Alice* was a quarter mile away already, moving steadily. The blazing gasoline slick around the patrol boat whumped and went out.

There was sudden shouting aboard the *Alice*. A fiery track shot skyward. As the flare reached the top of its arc and began a slowburning descent beneath a parachute he saw Margaret throwing life rings over the taffrail.

"Bet you can't catch me," Lilly taunted, and began an overhand crawl.

The *Alice* was taking in sail and starting to turn.

Foiled again! Through some temporal looping quirk Lilly was no longer disabled or drugged. Joe could never catch the weapons man and drag him down before he reached the *Alice*. He sighed. If Lilly was not going to cooperate there was no point in a solo suicide. Joe began swimming. A wave came from an unexpected angle and he swallowed salt water. The *Alice* was farther away than he had realized. Far enough to remind Joe that he was older now, short of breath, and not really cut out for this kind of crap.

Somebody fired another flare. "Some days," Joe growled, "You just can't make a dime." But his body, with its usual perversity, refused to give up. He got another mouthful of salt water but he continued swimming.

Lilly was already wringing his clothes out when Gorson leaned over the rail to help Joe aboard. "Wish you'd make up your mind," the weapons man said with that tight smile that haunted Joe's dreams.

Joe tried to remember if this was exactly what Lilly had said the last time—the time he'd pulled the log line in.

"Captain!" It was Howard Hennis. The gangling black seemed worried. "You seen Kraus?"

Why ask me? Have I been minding the store? Then Joe saw what else was going to be different in this time loop. Would he never be rid of Lilly? He went below. Cook and Dr. Greybull were shaking their heads. Freedy glanced at Joe and became busy holding his broken glasses together. Margaret studied Joe with a hint of tears.

"Did I forget to zip my fly?" Joe asked.

"Raquel's gone," Cook said. "Her Injuns too."

"Why not? Everything else has gone wrong." Would Raquel have landed back in her village with her family? Which family? The one in tenth century Spain or with her sons and grandsons in sixteenth century Mexico? She had been fished from the sea by these Indians—which blew a few holes in Dr. Greybull's sympathetic magic theory of time travel.

Some corner of his mind kept telling Joe that he should react. His meddling had taken Raquel out of her own time and had dumped her into the sea where only luck had saved her. This time—even if she were rescued promptly, how much exposure could an old woman endure? Why couldn't her life had ended serenely, surrounded by her children?

And Kraus? There had not been time for Lilly to do him in. And in this time frame—abruptly Joe understood the boy's tranquil manner that night when Lilly had gone overboard. Kraus had not done it! Neither had Joe—that time. Who had? Abruptly Joe rushed back on deck. He bent over the rail and vomited several liters more sea water than he had swallowed.

Margaret was hanging on lest he go over the rail again. "I'm sorry," she said.

"Don't apologize. You've done nothing to regret. I have."

"What?"

Joe faced the man who had told him never to apologize. Gorson and Cook hovered in the background. "Arrest him," Joe said. "Keelhaul him if he gives you an excuse. Just see that he never gets loose again."

"But—" Margaret changed her mind.

"If the *Alice* goes down Lilly goes with her," Joe said.

"Yes, sir!" Gorson was positively cheerful.

Lilly had already changed into dry clothes and was exuding an aura of Wild Turkey. He grinned. "No hard feelings, I hope,'' he said as Gorson and Cook began binding his hands behind him.

"No," Joe said thoughtfully. "Through inattention I may have contributed, but the paradise we now inhabit is largely your doing. I can think of nothing more appropriate than that you be condemned to life."

Lilly grinned again. "Man and cockroach are marvelously adaptive animals. We survive."

Dr. Greybull, Freedy, Gorson and Cook were witnessing this exchange. Margaret came below, followed by Hennis.

"You know," Cook observed, "Pistolilly here's been out for a while. Bet he don't know what happened."

"Nothing that cannot unhappen," the weapons man said. "If the future is as grim and foreboding as you paint it then we must go back and change it."

"To something worse?" Joe asked. There was a sudden cramp in his midsection. For an instant he thought he was going to vomit more ocean but it was just his stomach reminding him of Raquel.

"Where you want to put him?" Cook asked. By now Lilly's hands were secured behind him with a trussing that ran to his ankles. If he lay quiet he could exist in reasonable comfort. Straining at the knots would give the weapons man a painful reminder that the *Alice's* crew retained the marlinspike skills of an earlier era.

Joe considered. There were no bunks to spare. He didn't want a bound prisoner playing skeleton at the feast from the galley settee. It seemed sacrilege to put him in what had once been Raquel's domain but there was no other place. "Stuff him in the chain locker."

Joe wanted to retreat to his cabin and sort things out. He had tried to murder Lilly. He had arrested the man who had saved his life several times. Was Lilly right? Would they really remember him as part of the good old days 'when the Russians take over'? He remembered the man who had asked, "Who the hell are they?"

He watched as Gorson and Cook installed the security

expert in the chain locker, then turned to Freedy. "I've lost all track," Joe confessed. "Where and when are we?"

"That guy on the radio thought it was nineteen ninety four." Freedy clapped a hand to his forehead in time to rescue his glasses. "Nope," he amended. "We jumped since then. Hell, I don't know. That patrol boat burning—I guess we're back in the bootlegging twenties again.

And the man who called himself the United States Government had never heard of the Russians. What had they done to the time stream?

Dr. Greybull was struggling for Joe's attention. "Not right away," he said.

"What?"

"We can't try another time jump."

"Why not?"

"Rose has cobbled up a wind charger and he still uses that little gasoline generator but it takes forever. He's scrubbed the muck off the solar collectors. It all helps but we'll need several hours of wind and maybe a little sun before we'll have enough batteries to try anything."

Joe went on deck. "Freedy?" he called, "What's with fathometer and radar?"

"Sixteen fathoms and it's either a scattering layer or soft bottom," the radioman said. "There's land or maybe just clouds about a hundred miles east."

"Drop anchor," Joe said. "The wind charger will work faster."

They had to remove the trussed-up weapons man from the chain locker before they could drop anchor but finally it was done and he was back. Rose studied an ammeter and seemed satisfied with what he saw. Joe wished he knew what to do.

The past that he knew was gone. The future he and Lilly had created was infinitely worse. Would it turn out still worse if they were to jump backward and tinker once more with time?

He went up on deck and stared into the wind and darkness. The *Alice* rode easily and the wind charger whirred. He stood in Raquel's favorite refuge alone in the bows—where she had sat in long converse with Margaret, and Kraus interpreting. Why had Kraus disappeared? Descendant of Raquel? Something so infinitesimal as Baakot being away from home during a wife's fertile period? Time would never tell.

"Is there anything I can do?" It was Margaret.

"You can quit worrying about me."

"I'm sorry."

"Don't apologize."

"You said that."

Joe sighed. "Look," he finally said. "I'm sorry I made such a botch of things. I should never have stayed in the navy. If we could live our lives over I'm sure we'd all do some editing."

Margaret stared into the night. "I'd like to be off the hook for murder but I'm not really sorry for what I did. What would you change?"

"Occupational disease," Joe mumbled.

"What?"

"I was never really cut out for the navy. Should have gone back to teaching."

"Why?"

"Historians live in the past. I've abmicturated my life for a past that never was. So now we face a future that never will be."

"How?"

Don't explain. You'll just make it worse.

But Margaret would not let it alone. "What do you mean?"

"I suppose I knew all the time. I was just too bound up in my own miseries to notice until Raquel pointed it out to me." Joe turned and looked at his yeoperson. "Why did you do it?"

"Do what?"

"You've done my paperwork and you've saved my life. For your unswerving loyalty I sometimes buy you dinner and a drink. I'm gaining weight but I make up for it by losing my hair. What do you get out of it?"

"You're not some pimply kid who can't keep his hands off."

"I'm sorry," Joe said.

"For what?"

"For keeping my hands off!" Joe recalled all the idle hours he had run stress analyses on pantyhose from across an office. The years he had wasted for a dream. "I should have asked you to marry me. Would have if you'd ever turned on the pressure."

"I know."

"You're right," he said. "It never works when a man feels he's been trapped."

"I'm sleepy," Margaret said. "You using the bunk?"

"Go ahead."

"Those batteries won't be up before daylight, will they?"

Joe supposed they would not.

"It's a fairly wide bunk."

Joe was silent a long moment. "Did Raquel tell you to say that?'"

Margaret hesitated. "Yes."

When she had struggled to arrange his disordered life had Raquel known Joe's final bungle was going to kill her?

It was too soon. He was doing it all wrong. But captains should not have to sneak around—even in normal times. *Don't apologize. Don't explain.* There were times when Lilly could turn a phrase. "I'll be there in a minute," Joe said.

"I suppose I should feel excited—all trembly inside." Margaret gave a brittle laugh.

My God, I'm even botching this! Abruptly Joe grabbed his yeoperson and kissed her. "I'm excited," he said. She laughed again and this time he sensed it was going to be all right. She strode aft down the darkened deck and went below.

Joe stood facing into the wind and praying he could at last do something right. The wind charger whirred, pumping juice into the batteries. Was it really possible to go back and repair the damage Lilly had done the time stream?

He had spent over a minute mooning alone up here. It would not do to keep Margaret waiting. He strode sternward and lowered himself down the cabin slide, blinking in the sudden light.

Margaret was still not even in his cabin. Joe squinted and saw Freedy face down on the deck, his already-broken glasses scattered. Dr. Greybull lay pale and breathing shallowly beside him. But Joe took all this in only peripherally. His attention focussed on Dr. Lilly.

There were rope welts on the weapons man's wrists but there was no rope. While all hands snored the sleep of the emotionally drained, Dr. Lilly was tuning the time machine with one hand while the other pointed a pistol at Yeoperson Margaret White.

Joe was still only halfway down the cabin slide, still blinking. *You're not going to screw this up* he decided, and dived straight for Lilly's midsection.

Totally unsurprised, Dr. Lilly whacked Joe on the back of the neck.

Chapter 23

Joe came to crumpled in a corner of the galley. His shoulders were numb. From the neck up he was suffused with a terminal ache. After a moment found he could still move. The weapons man had not paralyzed him. Nor had Lilly regarded him dangerous enough to tie up. Margaret knelt beside him. Where in hell was everybody? His own fault. Joe knew he should have set a full watch but, riding at anchor a hundred miles offshore what was the point of depriving exhausted men of sleep?

Still, for men to sleep through all this bumping and thumping . . . He had a sudden suspicion. "Did you add a pinch of something to improve Cook's stew?"

"To get rid of the sniffles," Lilly said absently as he tuned the time machine.

Joe puzzled for a moment, then realized that everyone had suddenly gotten over the coughing and hacking that Baakot had brought aboard. Opium might be objectionable but it was great for drying up runny noses. "Haven't you done enough damage?" Joe asked.

"Too much," Lilly agreed. The planes and angles of his fanatical face skewed into a grin. "A responsible man admits his mistakes and tries to make amends."

"And each try puts us deeper in dreck."

"Maximum effort," Lilly said. "Ready or not, here we go." He flipped the switch.

"There isn't enough power yet—" Margaret began when they sensed the abrupt shimmer of a time jump. Joe braced himself for the bump of dry land or the inevitable landing a hundred feet above or below sea level that had to happen sooner or later. The *Alice* continued sailing smoothly. The darkness outside the portholes remained unchanged. He wondered if the weakened batteries had limited their jump to a few minutes.

Joe wanted to reassure Margaret but he knew that no matter what happened, it would only turn out worse. He studied Lilly, seeing some missing half of himself. If only he had possessed Dr. Lilly's assurance. If the weapons man had ever once doubted his own infallibility . . . If . . .

Something strange was happening. Joe blinked and struggled to clear his eyes from aftereffects of the chop on his neck. His head ached with the terminal ferocity of a bachelor's dinner hangover but his vision was clear. He had no trouble seeing a great grabbable area of dungarees where Margaret knelt beside him.

But Lilly was—attenuating. Joe had seen something like this once before, when Lilly and Fyodor-Theodore wrestled for the crozier that had nearly electrocuted the weapons man. Lilly showed vague alarm and surprise. Were the *Alice* and her people fading away from him too?

"He's—who's that behind him?" Margaret gasped.

"It's Theodore."

Still fingering his crozier, the bishop who had fished them from the sea was fading in behind Lilly.

"Who?" Margaret asked.

Joe shook his head and immediately wished he hadn't. Of the *Alice's* people only he and Lilly had ever seen Theodore.

Joe arrived at a sudden conclusion that the Council of Nicaea had not turned out exactly as Lilly and his silenced pistol had intended.

Lilly's knowing grin flashed. Then he sensed that neither Joe nor his yeoperson were attempting some simpleminded 'look behind you'. He turned just as the bishop aimed his crozier. Then Lilly and Theodore both faded into the realm of the Cheshire cat. Just before the bishop attenuated into nothingness he winked.

Joe and Margaret stared in shocked silence. Freedy moaned and tried to find his shattered glasses. Dr. Greybull was still breathing.

"Are you all right?" Margaret asked.

"I've got a headache," Joe said.

Margaret's concern dissolved into an impish grin as she watched Joe realize what he had just said. Then they were both howling with hysterical laughter.

"What the hell's going on?" Gorson emerged from the fo'c's'l clad in skivvy drawers. From his bleary look Joe knew he had been right about the opium. He considered the bleak despair that had enveloped him for most of this voyage and knew this was not the first time Lilly had experimented with mood-altering chemicals. No wonder Joe had turned into a superklutz! How long to flush the crap out of his system?

Margaret grinned and Joe struggled not to succumb to the giggles. "Lilly just jumped ship," he finally managed.

"You deep-sixed him for good?"

"If there are penalties for false confession then his sins caught up with him."

"What woke me up?" Gorson demanded. "Did we jump again?"

Joe forced himself to his feet. "We did. And somebody jerked Lilly out of the time stream just like—" He made himself say it. "Like Raquel."

Margaret was already fiddling with the radio. There was the machinegun stutter of a teletype signal coming over audio. She moved off it and picked up somebody punching out a hesitant cw. Then she had a voice in some language Joe thought was oriental.

"It's 1976," Freedy said an hour later. He too had a headache and his glasses were beyond holding together.

"Only ten years before we left." Gorson said.

"What's Watergate?" Freedy asked.

"There's one in the Tower of London," Dr. Greybull said. "Back when roads weren't too good most of the traffic was up and down the river."

"That water gate," Joe added, "was also a handy place to dump garbage. Traitors and anybody else with bald shoulders got flung out—preferably on a falling tide so the bodies wouldn't float upriver."

"That don't make sense," Freedy said.

"The reasons were both sanitary and political," Joe said. "Dead men tell no tales but the news of their death sometimes does."

"I mean Watergate," Freedy said. "They talk like it was worse than Teapot Dome."

"We can figure it out later," Joe said. "See if you can get me a time tick."

Moments later Joe had set his watch and was out in the cockpit. He locked the sextant and took it toward his cabin to work out their position.

"Hey Joe!" Gorson said. "They've two or three presidents in the last couple of years."

Joe felt a wrench in his viscera. If the Imperial Presidency had degenerated into South American musical chairs they might as well set up in business for themselves. Could he cut it as a pirate? Had Lilly left enough weapons? He turned on the light, which was very dim now, and began punching the sextant's reading into the calculator. When he had written it down he went out and asked Freedy for another time tick.

The radioman picked up the Arlington Observatory signal and Joe reset his watch. He had only been a second off, which resulted in less than a quarter mile error at this latitude. He went on deck and took his sights again. If he was extrapolating correctly from the tables he had for ten years ahead of this time, the *Alice* was less than 40 miles from San Diego. He wished there was enough battery left to try the radar.

"Do we go in?" Gorson asked? "Or do we sail in circles out here and try to figure out where we stand?"

"Where can we stand ten years before—" Dr. Greybull fingered the bandage on the back of his head and winced. "What if we meet ourselves—our families again?"

Joe thought back to that conference in Washington when he had met the Director who so resembled an older version of Lilly. The Director and the Imperial President seemed nearly forgotten. Bits of news and commentary they had been able to pick up seemed to refer to different people. He came to a sudden decision. "We go in."

"How?" Cook asked.

"The *Alice* was once a civilian yacht. Paint out a few things and she will be again. As long as we don't wear uniforms that're probably wrong for this time stream anyway—from now on it's dungarees."

"But what about customs?"

"A hundred yachts sail in and out every day. Customs may board us but if we haven't any exotic agricultural products aboard—" Joe paused and made a mental note to scour the *Alice* for Lilly's stash. "If we don't make waves I can go ashore and spend a couple of quiet days in a library—find out if we really want to stay."

"Can't we get back to our own time?" Hennis asked.

"After what we've done to screw up the time stream there isn't any time of our own. We're lucky to find this. Where's Kraus?" *Where's Raquel?* "Which of us disappears next time we jump?"

"Even to an old man," Greybull conceded, "your argument is compelling."

"Looks like you've got the weather for it," Rose said. "Look behind us."

The familiar 'night and morning fog and low clouds' of the SoCal forecast was moving in on them. The rosiness of this situation was marred only by the also familiar and total lack of wind after dark.

"I don't suppose there's the slightest hope of motoring?" Joe asked.

Rose shook his head.

Gorson posted watches and Joe settled down to listen to the radio. He learned more than he cared to know about bargains for $29.95, and nothing of what awaited them ashore. He awoke to a preacher's warning that only a constant cash flow could stay God's hand. It was 0900 before the *Alice* heeled to the first faint puff.

"Spinnaker?" Gorson asked.

"Check first with Rose about that backstay."

"It's fixed," Gorson said.

Joe turned to Freedy. "Batteries up enough now for the radar?"

Freedy nodded and fumbled without his glasses. After triangulation, Joe concluded that wind and current had drifted them ten miles closer overnight. It was 1400 before he saw the faint Gibraltarlike silhouette of Point Loma loom ghostly through fog.

Hennis spotted the buoy and they began sailing up the channel.

"Oh oh!" Gorson muttered.

Joe was inclined to agree. They had passed the bottleneck of Ballast Point and were within a couple of miles of the yacht basin. If the fog would just hold they could lose themselves among the several thousand yachts of this busy port. By some judicious moving about they could stay lost for weeks.

But the fog was lifting.

As the sun burned off the last of it Joe saw the familiar Coast Guard stripe on a boat drifting dead ahead. "Don't panic," he warned. "We've just come down from uh— Monterey sounds about right." Then he suddenly remembered. "Did you find that stuff Lilly's been putting in the soup?"

Gorson stared at Joe, then slapped a hand to his forehead.

"That why I been feeling so dopey? What was that sucker jerking us around for?"

"Beats me," Joe said. "But if you didn't find it, let us pray most devoutly that they can't either."

As the fog burned off Joe discovered that the bay was full of small boats. Half of them had cameras. Every boat had binoculars. Behind the boat with the Coast Guard stripe was a smaller cabin cruiser with two men and handheld TV cameras on the pulpit. Joe had a sudden feeling that he was never going to make it quietly ashore to the library.

"Waitin' for us!" Cook said.

There was room to turn but it would take time to strike the spinnaker and—what was the use? Even with batteries at full charge the *Alice* was not going to outrun a Coast Guard patrol boat. Joe began rehearsing his story, praying they would not find wherever Lilly had stashed his dope. Then he remembered the arms cache. How to explain that?

Had Lilly laid this trap for them?

A band emitted some preliminary tootles and began playing. A fireboat began squirting the harbor skyward in a vain attempt to circumvent gravity. Small boats were sounding whistles and bells.

This was the kind of welcome reserved for aircraft carriers after a particularly arduous tour of duty. Joe looked behind in sudden panic. Was he about to be run down?

There was nothing behind the *Alice*.

The Coast Guard came alongside just as Gorson dropped the spinnaker. As the *Alice* lost way a man grasped a stay and swung aboard. He wore the stripes of a captain. "Welcome home," he declaimed. "Welcome to the heroes who singlehandedly sunk a sub and sent an unmistakable message to terrorists throughout the world."

Joe stared. The man in captain's uniform winked. The last time Joe had seen that wink this captain had been holding a bishop's crozier. Joe noted that the captain's stripes were accompanied by the cross of a Christian chaplain. "Theodore?" He still was not sure.

"It's him!" Margaret exclaimed. "The same man that—"
The bishop-captain gave her a warning look.

I may be slow, Joe thought, *but sooner or later I get the message.* The bishop had been clueing them in to respond properly to all the cameras and reporters.

He glanced at the Coast Guard boat. Nobody in hearing distance. Oblivious of possible parabolic mikes on other boats, Joe spoke in the koine they had used at the Council. "What did you do with Lilly?" he hissed.

"Welcome home, heroes," Theodore said. "I'm not sure to what you refer but I'm sure it never happened."

Before Joe could pursue the subject he was facing microphones and interviewers. "Nothing really," he managed. "Just doing our duty."

The remainder of the *Alice's* people stared with closed mouths and growing horror.

"Sheeit!" Cook muttered. "Wish I uz home!"

Epilogue

A week had passed and, in spite of headaches and other obstacles Joe and Margaret were on a different footing now. She handled the paperwork with her usual efficiency. Bishop-captain Theodore, who had turned out regular navy instead of Coast Guard, had been most helpful.

Those of the *Alice's* crew with families had been given leave and had gone home in a state of intense curiosity. While the *Alice* underwent repairs and refitting, the others were quartered in barracks or ashore. Joe and Margaret shared an efficiency apartment in walking distance of the base.

Joe had spent most of his time reading back copies of Time and Newsweek. There was a tantalizing almostness to this time stream. There had been an Imperial President and there had been a Director. One look at the bulldogfaced faggot of a Director and Joe thought he knew what had happened to Lilly. The weapons man's tempollution had wiped out a probability and Lilly had never been born.

Watergate . . . It troubled Joe that he was, in some degree, responsible for having created the conditions that broke this scandal but . . . had he been all that happy with unrestrained repression and the Imperial Presidency?

He still could not fathom Bishop-Captain Theodore-Fyodor's role. Lilly had planted himself and Joe where the bishop's ship would rescue them. Had Lilly known then that Theodore was not all he seemed to be? If the bishop had really been working to restore the Tsar . . . Joe shrugged. Even without the the shah's increasingly stern warnings the Soviet Union seemed to be having new troubles each day feeding the growing expectations of hungry citizens who no longer *believed*.

There was that strange resemblance between Lilly and a Watergate conspirator with a penchant for holding his hand over burning candles. But again, nothing was quite right.

It had been a trying time for Americans when their Imperial President screwed up so badly that he was driven to plea bargaining with a second string bungler. But Joe knew he was going to be happier here than back in his old time stream. Might as well be. He could no more go back than he could find a young Raquel again. And if he had—what kind of a navy officer's wife could he have expected out of 10th century Spain?

Things were working out. Margaret thought so too. There might be a few problems but Jimmy Carter could handle them.

H. BEAM PIPER

☐ 24890	**FOUR DAY PLANET/LONE STAR PLANET**	$2.25
☐ 26192	**FUZZY SAPIENS**	$1.95
☐ 48492	**LITTLE FUZZY**	$1.95
☐ 26193	**FUZZY PAPERS**	$2.75
☐ 49053	**LORD KALVAN OF OTHERWHEN**	$2.25
☐ 77779	**SPACE VIKING**	$2.25
☐ 23188	**FEDERATION (5¼'' x 8¼'')**	$5.95

ACE SCIENCE FICTION
P.O. Box 400, Kirkwood, N.Y. 13795

S-10

Please send me the titles checked above. I enclose _____.
Include 75¢ for postage and handling if one book is ordered; 50¢ per book for two to five. If six or more are ordered, postage is free. California, Illinois, New York and Tennessee residents please add sales tax.

NAME_____

ADDRESS_____

CITY_____STATE_____ZIP_____

Classic stories by America's most distinguished and successful author of science fiction and fantasy.

ANDRE NORTON

"Nobody can top Miss Norton when it comes to swashbuckling science fiction adventure stories." —*St. Louis Globe-Democrat*

07897	**Breed to Come**	$1.95
14236	**The Defiant Agents**	$1.95
22376	**The Eye of the Monster**	$1.95
24621	**Forerunner Foray**	$2.25
66835	**Plague Ship**	$1.95
78194	**Star Hunter/Voodoo Planet**	$1.95
81253	**The Time Traders**	$1.95

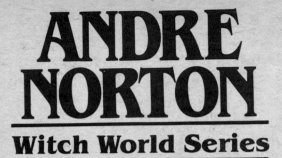

ANDRE NORTON

Witch World Series

Enter the Witch World for a feast of adventure and enchantment, magic and sorcery.

89705	**Witch World**	$1.95
87875	**Web of the Witch World**	$1.95
80805	**Three Against the Witch World**	$1.95
87323	**Warlock of the Witch World**	$1.95
77555	**Sorceress of the Witch World**	$1.95
94254	**Year of the Unicorn**	$1.95
82356	**Trey of Swords**	$1.95
95490	**Zarsthor's Bane** (illustrated)	$1.95

Available wherever paperbacks are sold or use this coupon.

MORE TRADE SCIENCE FICTION

Ace Books is proud to publish these latest works by major SF authors in deluxe large format collectors' editions. Many are illustrated by top artists such as Alicia Austin, Esteban Maroto and Fernando.

Robert A. Heinlein	Expanded Universe	21883	$8.95
Frederik Pohl	Science Fiction: Studies in Film (illustrated)	75437	$6.95
Frank Herbert	Direct Descent (illustrated)	14897	$6.95
Harry G. Stine	The Space Enterprise (illustrated)	77742	$6.95
Ursula K. LeGuin and Virginia Kidd	Interfaces	37092	$5.95
Marion Zimmer Bradley	Survey Ship (illustrated)	79110	$6.95
Hal Clement	The Nitrogen Fix	58116	$6.95
Andre Norton	Voorloper	86609	$6.95
Orson Scott Card	Dragons of Light (illustrated)	16660	$7.95

Available wherever paperbacks are sold or use this coupon.

ACE SCIENCE FICTION
P.O. Box 400, Kirkwood, N.Y. 13795

Please send me the titles checked above. I enclose _____.
Include 75¢ for postage and handling if one book is ordered; 50¢ per book for two to five. If six or more are ordered, postage is free. California, Illinois, New York and Tennessee residents please add sales tax.

NAME_____

ADDRESS_____

CITY_____STATE_____ZIP_____

S-15

Gordon R. Dickson

☐	16015	Dorsai!	1.95
☐	34256	Home From The Shore	2.25
☐	56010	Naked To The Stars	1.95
☐	63160	On The Run	1.95
☐	68023	Pro	1.95
☐	77417	Soldier, Ask Not	1.95
☐	77765	The Space Swimmers	1.95
☐	77749	Spacial Deliver	1.95
☐	77803	The Spirit Of Dorsai	2.50

Available wherever paperbacks are sold or use this coupon.

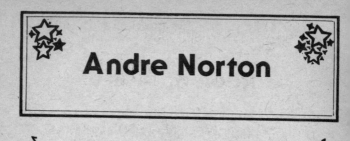

Andre Norton

☐ 12314	Crossroads Of Time	$1.95
☐ 16664	Dragon Magic	1.95
☐ 33704	High Sorcery	1.95
☐ 37291	Iron Cage	1.95
☐ 45001	Knave Of Dreams	1.95
☐ 47441	Lavender Green Magic	1.95
☐ 67556	Postmarked The Stars	1.25
☐ 71100	Red Hart Magic	1.95
☐ 78015	Star Born	1.75

Available wherever paperbacks are sold or use this coupon.